PATH OF RESISTANCE

ROOK WINTERS

*For my father, the only person who drops references to
my stories into conversations*

CHAPTER 1

Ainsley was ready to open the valve on the old fuel tank when Jasmine waved at her to stop.

"I've got something better."

She pulled a silver block from her pack, peeled away a strip from one edge, and pressed the block against the fuel tank.

"What's that?"

"A pop box. It'll make a lot more of a mess than just opening the valve."

Ainsley grabbed her by the wrist. "An explosive? Are you insane? That's not the plan."

"The plan is underwhelming." She tapped the pop box with her free hand. "This is going to make a statement."

"What statement? Two found dead in the wreckage of a blown up warehouse?"

Jasmine pulled her wrist free. "I'm not an idiot. It's on a

timer, and I have an app on my bracelet. I can detonate or disarm it any time."

"Even if we get away, that kind of damage means an investigation. They'll come looking for us. No one's going to bother if a shipment gets damaged by some leaking fuel."

"That's the problem. It doesn't hurt them if they don't feel it. They'll feel this."

"Jasmine, please, think for a second..."

"You said you were serious about hitting the Qyntarak. We've always agreed the goal is to hurt them."

"Yes, but that—"

"But nothing. This is how we hurt them. End of discussion. Come on, we need to go."

Ainsley wanted to protest but she didn't know what else to say. She wasn't in charge. They had an informal partnership at best. There was no chain of command, no rules for resolving disputes in the field. And Jasmine was right about needing to go. The warehouse had two guards on duty who could show up at any moment.

Human guards...

The implication dawned on her.

"The security guards. You'll kill them."

"They're collaborators. They deserve to die."

"We hit Qyntarak, not people."

"We can have this debate later. The timer's set for fifteen minutes. We need to leave."

Without waiting for a reply, Jasmine pulled the straps of her pack tight and ran to a rope ladder hanging from what used to be a window. Ainsley looked back at the unassuming pop box. Volatile liquid fuels weren't common. A small explosion would trigger a massive reaction. It was a rare opportunity.

She followed Jasmine.

Under normal circumstances, they'd pull the ladder up behind themselves, minimizing the evidence they were leaving behind. There was no point tonight. But they really needed to get some distance between themselves and the warehouse before it turned into a fireball.

It took a couple minutes to reach their egress point, a hole they'd made in the perimeter fence that wrapped around a dozen warehouse buildings to keep out vandals and poorly motivated thieves. Except the hole wasn't there.

"What the hell?" Jasmine dropped to her knees.

"This isn't the right spot. We must have taken a wrong turn."

"No, this is it. The fence has been repaired." Jasmine touched a barely noticeable spot where the metal of the links reflected the moonlight a little brighter than elsewhere.

Ainsley leaned in closer, not believing what she was seeing. Before she could put her disbelief into words, everything around them was illuminated and a voice called out, "Don't move."

Despite the command, Ainsley twisted her torso to look. A guard was approaching with his stun gun drawn. Lights shone down from overhead, probably coming from two or three drones.

"On your knees. Hands on your heads. Now."

Ainsley looked at Jasmine, who was already kneeling in front of the fence. Jasmine tapped on her bracelet computer. The oblivious guard had just grabbed Ainsley's left wrist when the boom came. A brighter, yellower light engulfed everything, followed by a rush of warm air carrying an acrid smell.

The guard swore and Ainsley used the distraction to pull her arm free. She rolled with the momentum and landed on her back. As the guard turned on her, she drove her foot between his legs and he stumbled sideways.

Ainsley clambered to her feet. Jasmine already had the guard's stun gun in her hand. She fired a slug into him and he convulsed before collapsing, moaning as he cupped his crotch with one hand and pressed the other to the slug's point of impact.

Jasmine adjusted the gun's settings and fired again. The man shook as he lost consciousness. His head rolled to one side and the lights from the drones shifted to illuminate the area where he would be looking if he were awake.

"Now we really have to move." Jasmine tossed the gun aside and started up the old chain-link fence.

"There's razor wire up there."

"A little razor wire never hurt anyone."

"Pretty sure the exact opposite is true."

"Relax. I'll cut away a section. It's faster than making a new hole in the fence."

Ainsley wasn't convinced but Jasmine had the cutters and was a third of the way up already. Over it would be.

The fence rattled and shook as they climbed. A length of razor wire fell to the ground as Ainsley climbed. Jasmine snipped and tossed more segments until there was an opening wide enough for them to go one at a time.

Jasmine swung over first and made good time going down. When Ainsley went over, her pack snagged. She told herself not to panic as she shifted her weight but she couldn't pull herself free.

"Hurry up."

"My bag is caught."

"Leave it."

"It has my take in it."

"It's not worth getting caught over."

She was right, Ainsley knew. The few low value items they'd salvaged from the warehouse would pay rent for a week, if that. That was secondary to striking the Qyntarak. Even so, she hated to lose it all. Grunting as she did it, Ainsley pulled the knife from her boot. With a white-knuckled, one-handed grip on the fence, she cut away the straps. When the second strap let go, her weight shifted and she almost fell. She stabbed at the bottom of the pack with the dim hope that she could cut it open and something valuable enough to carry would fall out.

From below, Jasmine's voice was strained. "Three seconds and I'm leaving without you."

Ainsley exhaled in defeat, sheathed the knife, and started down. She jumped the last six feet, landing in a crouch, and chased after Jasmine into the sparse woods that separated the warehouses from the edge of the city.

Without a pack weighing her down, Ainsley was gaining when the unmistakable hum of a grav flyer passed over them. The inhuman form of a Qyntarak dropped through the trees, landing less than twenty feet from Jasmine. Both women slid to a stop. The creature used its six tentacles to steady itself as it found its footing on the four scorpion-like legs that held up its elongated body.

Ainsley jumped sideways, taking cover behind the nearest trunk.

The alien was at least seven feet tall and towered over

Jasmine. With a swipe of one of its longest tentacles, it took Jasmine's feet out from under her and she hit the ground with a gasp. The end of a tentacle clamped around her throat and pinned her down.

Its synthetic, translated voice played from a speaker in its body armor. "Human, your actions are foolish. You bring shame to yourself. The costs for your crime will be great."

The raspy reply from Jasmine was indecipherable.

"Additional human, much wisdom exists in revealing your location. Delay of capture results only in greater expense."

Ainsley tightened her hands into fists. They had a plan for this. If one of them was captured, the other was not to give herself up, even with the promise for leniency. If they were both taken, neither would talk. The arrangement had seemed simple enough when they'd come up with it. Now, Ainsley was having second thoughts. How was she supposed to help Jasmine once she was taken? And how, in good conscience, could she stand by and do nothing while her partner was taken away to some unknown location?

"Do not welcome more consequence, additional human. The opportunity is now for lowest cost."

"Back to the farm, Bobby." That was their signal—a code for Jasmine to tell Ainsley that she was going to create a distraction and for Ainsley to take the opportunity to escape.

Ainsley squeezed her eyes tight for a moment, forcing away the tears that were building up. Even the fastest human couldn't outrun an average Qyntarak. Ainsley's only chance was a diversion that gave her enough time to get somewhere that her body heat would be shielded. And even then she would only be safe if there weren't others and if this one wasn't wearing enhanced sensors.

Ainsley chanced a look around the tree and saw Jasmine twist her body until she could pull out her knife and saw at the fabric of her backpack.

The Qyntarak's centipede-like body twisted and swiveled nearly 360 degrees, searching with its thermal optic nerve for Ainsley. When it swung in her direction, she pulled her head back. When she looked again, the monster's body was still pointing her way. It had spotted her and was probably deciding how to catch her without losing Jasmine. Although the creature was three or four times her body weight, physics dictated that dragging Jasmine would slow it down.

But Ainsley hadn't needed to worry. In the few seconds that the Qyntarak spent staring in Ainsley's direction, Jasmine peeled the cover off the adhesive backing of another pop box. She slapped it on the armor covering the Qyntarak's tentacle. This time there was no delay. A brilliant light flashed as a crack rang out like the sound of two boulders smashing together followed by the sounds of organic material smacking against the tree trunks.

A wailing roar came from the Qyntarak that sent shivers down Ainsley's spine. She looked again for a fraction of a second, long enough to see that much of one tentacle was gone.

On the ground were parts of what used to be Jasmine. Ainsley fought back the urge to vomit and forced herself to run. She went into a full sprint, confident the Qyntarak wouldn't hear her footfalls over the din it was making. She kept running as fast as her lungs and legs would let her until she'd cleared the woods and reached the first of a stretch of abandoned concrete homes.

They were utilitarian living quarters built decades earlier

to hold refugees when the sea levels rose. Ainsley kicked in the half-rotten wood door of the nearest entrance and hid inside long enough to catch her breath. The place stank of urine. Some small animal scurried away. It spooked her, but compared with the seven-foot alien, a rodent was quaint and almost familiar.

She felt like her heart was going to explode as she sucked air into her lungs. As soon as her fear outweighed the exhaustion, she returned to the night air and continued at a slower pace. She just had to get to a populated area. Being near other humans would be safer.

Sweat had soaked through her shirt when she found a thin beam of light leaking out through the curtains of what she guessed might be an after hours drinking establishment.

She knocked on the door and a man with an unkempt beard cracked it open.

"What do you want?"

"Help, please. Someone's trying to hurt me."

The man pulled the door open a little further and peered out into the street, which was empty save for Ainsley and quiet except for her ragged breathing.

"Alright, come in for a little while."

As she had guessed, the interior was a residential space converted to a makeshift saloon. A dozen or so men sat huddled in groups drinking from ancient-looking pint glasses. They were all men, which gave Ainsley some pause, but they were safer than a Qyntarak.

"You look awful frightened, girl."

"It's been a rough night. Thank you for letting me in."

"Well, I'm not a heartless monster. Hell knows we've got enough of them running the planet nowadays, don't we? You want a pint? Take the edge off?"

"I don't have a way to pay."

"Well, how about we say one is on the house? Consider it a small bit of restitution from my kind."

He waved his arms around the saloon, gesturing to the gaggle of men around them.

He assumes I was attacked by a man. That's probably best.

"Thank you."

She sipped her ale slowly, testing its potency and stretching out her time in the illusion of safety among the drinking men. There were cameras, drones, and flyers all over the city. If even a few of them had caught images of her, it wouldn't take long for the authorities to track her. Reflexively, she touched her cheek and hoped the facial deformers under her skin were doing their job.

A feeling of breathlessness gripped her and drove her to her feet. She returned the pint glass, still a third full, and thanked the bartender for his hospitality.

"Be safe out there, kid. Still a few hours until daylight."

"I will."

Before stepping out, she looked in all directions like the barkeeper had done earlier. The cold breeze cut through her still-damp clothes and drove a chill into her bones. She shivered and set out for home.

CHAPTER 2

THE ORIGINAL ESCAPE plan included an electric scooter stashed in the woods. Ainsley had sprinted past its hiding place. It wasn't until she was making the long walk back home that she even remembered the scooter.

She muttered a soft curse at herself. It would take her hours, well into daylight, to go the entire way on foot. She decided she'd find a black market taxi with a human driver who would be willing to wait while she went inside to fetch an anonymous currency token to pay her fare.

Ainsley preferred to keep an impenetrable wall between her extracurricular activities and her sanitized "real" life. Taking a car home from a job was letting the two worlds bleed into each other far too much for her liking. But what choice did she have?

It took another ninety minutes to reach an area where she could find a taxi. The driver was reluctant to take her the distance she requested with only the promise of an extra-large tip when they got there, but greed or pity ultimately won him over. He insisted on following her up the stairs and down the hallway to the little room she rented. It made Ainsley uncomfortable but any potential threat felt too small to fret about at the moment.

When she'd paid and sent him on his way, she locked her door and collapsed onto the tiny cot that served as her couch and bed. She closed her eyes to sleep but that was impossible.

The night replayed in a loop in her mind. The security guard lying unconscious on the ground, Jasmine held down by the Qyntarak, the gore after the pop box, and that alien wail...

She tried to control her breathing and force her body to relax, drawing on techniques her mother had taught her years ago, but it was no use. Her hands were cold and trembling.

She lifted the corner of her mattress and felt for the seam where she'd made a hiding spot for her few valuables. She rummaged inside until her hand found a small cylinder.

Popping off the cover, Ainsley used a shaky finger to slide out a single white tablet. She couldn't remember the names of the drugs that drove away everything, and tonight she could not have cared less. She swallowed, returned the container to its hiding place, and waited for the pill to do its work.

WHEN SHE WOKE, her windowless room gave no clues about the time of day. According to her bracelet computer, it was early evening. She'd slept for hours.

Then the memories of the night before rushed back and she couldn't breathe again.

"Jasmine..." she whispered.

Jasmine had sacrificed herself. That was never part of the deal. They'd done at least a dozen jobs together, but they hardly knew each other. She didn't even know Jasmine's real name. And Jasmine, or whoever she was, had given her life to save Ainsley's.

Grief and guilt swelled up and then fell away, each making room for the other over and over again, countless times in the span of a few moments. None of this was right. None of this was how things were supposed to go.

The walls of her ten-foot by twelve-foot room pulsed like they would squeeze in and crush her. Ainsley stood and tried to pace the floor but the room wasn't big enough.

Her legs hurt and her lips were parched. The scant mouthful left in her water jug wouldn't be enough for her dehydrated state. She'd have to go out.

While changing into fresh clothes, she remembered that she still needed to dispose of her clothing from the op, which had been their routine on all of their previous outings. That would have to wait. She freed her hair from tight braids and ran her fingers through it until she could pull it into a ponytail.

Outside, the sky was a dull gray and no brighter than it had been when she'd returned home that morning.

Her bracelet dinged the moment she stepped onto the street. An advertisement for a dinner special from a nearby restaurant.

World's gone to hell but at least the ads still work...

A girl's voice called out to her. "Miss Esther, you took out your nice braids I did for you."

Ainsley smiled at Raita, who was seven or maybe eight by now. The kids in the neighborhood told her when they had birthdays but there were too many of them for her to keep track.

"I did, but they were lovely. Well worth the price."

"Mama says she saw you come home tres early."

"Or tres late," one of the other kids said with a trill. "Did you meet a handsome man, hmm?"

Ainsley stuck her tongue out at the cluster of kids and winked. "A lady doesn't tell."

It was best if the kids made their own assumptions about the life and habits of Esther Rosenbaum, the name by which they knew her—the name her parents had given her. Suspicions about her activities could someday mean trouble for her or them. Or both.

The Common Table, one of her favorite spots to eat, promised a bustling scene through its dirty window, but Ainsley kept walking. She needed solitude and a few stiff drinks at more modest prices than she'd find there. A dozen blocks later, she ducked into a dingy-looking bar with only the word DRINKS scratched into its door.

The bartender raised an eyebrow at her request for a glass of water, two shots of his cheapest spirits, and a beer to chase them down, but he tapped a payment transceiver against her bracelet computer without a word and poured the drinks.

After a third shot and a second beer, the room was spinning enough to distract her from her thoughts. After her fourth beer, a man with a small gut and strong body odor tried to get too close to her. The details were fuzzy but

Ainsley was pretty sure she'd sucker punched the creep before the bartender asked him to leave.

Her fourth shot was courtesy of someone else, something Ainsley wouldn't have accepted when sober.

She didn't remember the rest of the evening.

CHAPTER 3

THE THRUMMING OF the air exchanger felt like it was boring into her brain. Ainsley pulled the pillow over her head and squeezed to no avail. With considerable effort, she slapped her right hand against her left wrist, groping for the button to activate voice control for her bracelet computer so she could check the time, but her computer wasn't there.

She gave a frustrated moan and shifted to her side. Her stomach felt sour. The smell of lemon and bleach wasn't helping with the nausea.

It took a dozen seconds before she realized that lemon and bleach were not normal smells in her room. It was several more seconds before she started to panic, threw the pillow from her head, and sat up.

The room wasn't hers. It was larger and much nicer. The furniture looked new and not scavenged.

Ainsley was relieved to find that she was clothed and her

bracelet computer was resting on a small table next to the bed. Trepidatiously, she touched the more intimate parts of her body, looking for signs of pain or injury. She seemed to be fine and felt normal other than the signs of an intense hangover that was going to haunt her all day.

As she fitted her bracelet computer back around her left wrist, she wondered what gracious soul had taken her in. Then a darker thought chilled her. What if someone had brought her here to sober her up? What if it wasn't altruism but a patient, violent lust? Some thug who didn't want a woman throwing up on him when he was forcing himself on her?

That pressed her into overdrive. She scanned the room to make sure she wasn't leaving anything behind and rushed for the door. It had an old-fashioned handle that, much to her relief, was unlocked.

She made it two steps before a woman blocked her path.

"Good morning, Ainsley. Welcome back to the land of the living."

"Who are you? Where am I?"

"Take it easy, you're fine."

"That's not an answer."

The woman, who was many years older and several inches taller than Ainsley, smiled down at her.

"If you'll slow down for a moment, I'll explain." The woman continued to smile and Ainsley couldn't decide if it was meant to be condescending or sinister. "But first how are you feeling?"

"I'm feeling like I want to know who you are and where I am."

The woman chuckled and clasped her hands together in

front of her.

"Fair enough. My name is Miriam. Or at least, you can call me Miriam, just like I can call you Ainsley. Instead of Esther Rosenbaum."

"How do you—"

"Let's leave the questions for a bit, shall we? I am, for lack of a better word, an entrepreneur. A friend referred me to you. I have a job that I believe might interest you."

"Which friend?"

"It doesn't matter. Nobody you know."

"How can—"

"I said it doesn't matter. It didn't take much sleuthing to track you down, but I seem to have found you in a bit of a distressing moment last night. You were, I must say, astonishingly drunk. A risky course of action, in my opinion, for a young woman out on the town by herself. You never know what kind of weirdo might take advantage of you in that state. Try to take you somewhere against your will."

"Yeah, what kind of weirdo..."

Miriam wagged her finger and a grin stretched across her face. "I see what you did there. I appreciate a sense of wit."

"How did I end up here? And where is this?"

"As I said, I found you quite drunk. I tried to engage you in conversation, even ordered us a round of the criminally poor quality alcohol at that bar, but I was overdressed for the venue. Not sure you remember any of this, but there was a steady stream of dreadfully overconfident admirers interrupting us. We didn't get much past civil introductions before you grew too tired and laid your head down on the bar. And fell asleep."

"So you decided to kidnap me?"

"Kidnap you? If I had left you passed out in that bar, you most likely would've woken up this morning in an alley, sore and bloody. That's a horror that never leaves you."

Ainsley considered the tall woman. Something about the way her words came out made Ainsley think she wasn't speaking in hypotheticals.

Miriam added, "We can't drink away our horrors, no matter how hard we try."

The women stared at each other until Ainsley shook her head, driving away the image of Jasmine's mangled body that had creeped into her thoughts. The sudden motion hurt like hell.

"Alright, thanks for the life advice. I'm not really in the market for a job right now, so I'll just see myself out. Is that the exit?"

Miriam didn't stop her, but as Ainsley's hand reached for the doorknob, the woman spoke again.

"I know where you were the night before last, Esther. I know what Ainsley was doing. I think you might find the work I have is aligned with your own interests. I'll respect your decision not to participate but will you at least do me the courtesy of hearing my proposal before you walk out?"

Ainsley's hand stopped an inch from the knob. In her mental fog, she'd hardly noticed that Miriam knew both her real name and her codename. Nobody knew about both of her worlds. Not even Jasmine had known her real name. Who was this woman?

"How do you know those names?" Ainsley spun around to face Miriam and the room kept spinning, causing her to stumble back, and she had to brace herself against the closed door.

"Why don't you sit down? I'll make you a cup of tea and my own personal hangover cure. We'll talk."

Miriam's hangover cure turned out to be a combination of hot sauce, whiskey, and the powdered contents of a pill that Miriam didn't identify. It didn't so much cure Ainsley's hangover as it distracted her from her hangover symptoms with different pain and suffering. She resisted several urges to throw up, but by the time Miriam set a hot cup of tea in front of her, Ainsley's stomach felt halfway normal.

"I have a job to do. And I need a confidence artist. The target is Qyntarak, not human. It's a simple plan. No one gets hurt and the take is spectacular. It's a slightly larger scale than the little outings you've been doing, but philosophically and ethically, it will be a perfect fit for you. From what I understand, the operations you've been executing have targeted Qyntarak resources with limited violence and little to no negative implications for humans. I like that. My friend who recommended you also appreciates it. I think it's the reason that you've been allowed to continue operating."

"Allowed? I don't asked anybody for their permission. I work independently."

"Not really independently. You did thirteen jobs in a row with someone you knew as Jasmine. My condolences, for what they're worth. It's hard to lose a colleague, no matter the circumstances."

"You need to tell me how you know so much about me."

Miriam smiled at her again. That same condescending smile. "You're going to have to accept that there are some things I'm not at liberty to divulge to you. I know that can be frustrating. I like answers and transparency as much as the next person, but there are bigger factors at play. You and I, we're doers. Bureaucrats, corporate executives, the elite, they sit in their meeting rooms and behind their desks and in their fortified homes and make decisions that impact the entire world, and when you're a pawn or a knight on the chessboard, you don't get the whole picture, you just have to play your part towards winning the bigger game."

Ainsley had heard of chess, but she'd never played and had no idea of the rules or mechanics of the game. Nevertheless, she thought she understood the metaphor. "You're saying that you're being used? You're a piece in someone else's game?"

"My dear, I'm no pawn. I am a willing participant. But it is, at the end of the day, a game. A game with the most serious stakes. If we want humanity to come out on top, we need players who can strike at the opponent in ways that really hurt. In ways that hurt a hell of a lot more than blowing up a single fuel tank."

Butterflies danced in Ainsley's stomach. She knew that this woman was intentionally triggering emotional responses. But knowing it intellectually didn't dampen the feelings. Ainsley was getting excited about the possibility of being involved in something bigger. It took restraint for her to not simply blurt out that she'd take the job, whatever it was.

She needed to give herself time to be rational about it.

"This all sounds tempting, but I need to think about it. How long before you need a decision?"

"I can give you a day. The wheels are already in motion for the operation. I can't afford delay. If you're not in, I must make other arrangements soon."

"How do I get in touch with you?"

"You won't have to. I'll get in touch with you."

"Tomorrow then."

Ainsley started to stand and Miriam placed a hand on Ainsley's as she pushed up from the table.

"Be careful, Ainsley. Whatever you decide, know that you will be at risk. The cameras and scanners at the facility you hit the other night have a record of you. It's only a matter of time now before they pick you up on one of the public cameras. When that happens, someone will show up unannounced and whisk you away. You don't want to end up paying off a lifetime's worth of fines aboard a red ship. It's no life. Trust me."

"I'll be fine. I was wearing a deformer and a signal scrambler. They'll never be able to find the real me."

"I'm afraid that's not true anymore. Aldebaran Industries has new capabilities that compensate for facial feature deforming technologies. Somewhere in one of their organic computers, they will calculate millions of variations of what you could look like without a deformer. It might take weeks, or even years, but they will find you."

"I've never heard of anything like that. You're just trying to scare me."

"I wish that were true. It's causing all of us to rethink our tactics."

Ainsley stood up straight and felt a knot tighten her stomach. If Miriam was speaking the truth, she was in trouble.

"I've arranged a series of transports to take you home via an indirect path. I'm sure you can appreciate the need for some precautions given our line of work. The first is an unlicensed, human-driven car waiting for you downstairs. The trip is prepaid. Just climb in and ask to go to Oz. The driver will know what to do."

The knot in Ainsley's stomach grew tighter as she left the apartment and made her way down one of the nicest hallways she'd ever seen. The building even had a functioning elevator that took mere seconds to deliver Ainsley from the seventh floor to ground level.

Whoever Miriam was, she didn't want for resources. And as much she hated to admit it to herself, that intrigued Ainsley.

CHAPTER 4

THE CIRCUITOUS ROUTE back to her neighborhood didn't give Ainsley much opportunity to reflect on the conversation with Miriam. The first driver left her at a loading dock where she was told to sit on a makeshift bench in the back of a delivery van that bounced and swerved on the rough streets on its way to a restaurant. From there, a boy pedaling an antique rickshaw took her to a public transit station, handed her an anonymous payment token, and told her to ride the train the rest of the way.

The train route didn't actually go near her neighborhood and Ainsley spent the better part of an hour walking from the transit station closest to her rented room.

Only when she was walking the final stretch through familiar streets was her mind able to focus on details. A large job that hurt the Qyntarak without human collateral damage. The idea was intoxicating. But what was the job? Blaming the effects from the previous night's binge and the disorienting effect of Miriam's so-called hangover cure, Ainsley lamented not asking more meaningful questions.

They wanted her for a con for something that would hurt Qyntarak. That wasn't much to go on. It was foolish to go in with total strangers who knew far too much about her. She had so little information and the potential for downside was unknown. For all she knew, they wanted to set her up to be the fall person for some outlandish operation.

It was a bad idea.

She needed to lie low, to just be Esther Rosenbaum for a while, to process the loss of Jasmine, and to find a new partner for the future. That was the safe thing to do. That was the smart thing.

Her confidence in her decision increased as she got closer to home.

She was almost there when she saw Raita and some other neighborhood kids playing in the street. They had stacked trash on an old cinderblock and were tossing a piece of mangled rebar at it like a spear with no hope of ever flying true.

As she drew nearer, their words became clear.

"Take that, alien scum."

"Go back to the dark, slimy ball of dirt you call home."

"Leave us alone, you monsters."

It wasn't an uncommon game, Ainsley knew. Still, the scene dredged up feelings of anxiety and unease. It was a slippery slope from play fighting with refuse to reckless encounters with real Qyntarak that would leave them imprisoned, injured, or worse.

The Qyntarak weren't violent oppressors. They didn't

have military control of the planet because they'd never needed it. They came with advanced technology and an offer to engage in commerce with Earth. Humanity had embraced them with open arms.

The trade relationship led to economic dominance that morphed into political control. It had never been overtly violent, but the threat was always lingering under the surface.

And then, as if Ainsley was walking in a living prophecy, the deep hum of a Qyntarak gravity control flyer emanated from somewhere in the distance behind her. For the briefest of moments, she feared they were coming for her. But when she saw the panic on the faces of the children, she shoved aside concerns for herself and started jogging toward the group.

"Come on, kids, let's go inside. Quickly now."

She pointed to an open archway in an abandoned section of what had once been a Greek restaurant. Half of the roof had collapsed at least a decade earlier but the front of the space was still useful for taking shelter if one was caught in some rain or snow. Or, in this case, if kids needed to get out of sight when a Qyntarak ship was flying overhead.

In her twenty-seven years, Ainsley had seen the Qyntarak come for a human in the street only once. That had been a long time ago. She'd just turned thirteen and one of the older teenagers had taken a bad hit of some homemade drug that sent him into a delirious rage. He had urinated on the steps of a government liaison office and then proceeded to throw rocks, sticks, and anything else he could get his hands on at the doors and windows of the single-story facility.

The little government building had housed administrators

and clerical staff. They had been trapped inside by the raging teenager. One of the parents had been lining up a stun gun to take the boy down when a grav flyer arrived. A Qyntarak in full body armor had raced out, and with a single jab of a tentacle to the side of the boy's head, had knocked him to the ground unconscious. They'd flown away with his body. The parents never saw him again. That one encounter cast a lasting shadow over their entire community and set thirteen-year-old Esther on a path of quiet resistance. Although it was a decade later before she adopted her codename, that had been the day Ainsley was born.

The design of Qyntarak grav flyers had not changed in the intervening years, and as Ainsley huddled with her arms around several of the whimpering children, she imagined the flyer from all those years ago as it descended to their street. But that didn't happen this time. The eerie hum of the flyer grew louder and then softer as it passed over and continued on its way. But it could return as fast as it had left so Ainsley waited until the sound was gone and then counted slowly to 100 to be certain.

When she finished counting, she released her grip on the children.

"Sounds like it's gone," she said. "It's safe to go back out."

One of the boys—Ainsley couldn't remember his name but thought he was Raita's younger cousin—looked up at her with wide eyes. "I don't like them," he whispered.

"No, me either."

"What if they come back?"

"I don't think they will. Not today. But if they come, you know what to do. Run inside to wait until they're gone. Remember, the aliens don't come looking for trouble from us. If you leave them alone, they'll leave you alone."

Ainsley left the children with an admonition that they play a game that didn't involve hurling insults at a mock alien. No one protested.

Back in her room, Ainsley lay on her cot and stared at the ceiling.

"If you leave them alone," she muttered to herself, "they'll leave you alone."

CHAPTER 5

Ainsley's small room felt even smaller than usual after Miriam's extravagant apartment. There wasn't much in her space other than her cot—just a minimal counter, old bins for clean and dirty clothes, and a single folding chair. She was out of food and had forgotten to replenish her water.

Her clothes from two nights earlier were still hidden behind the grate of the air vent. She put them at the bottom of the bag she used for hauling laundry and tossed a few other items on top.

Ainsley and Jasmine's routine had been to incinerate their clothes at the end of a mission, but her incendiary powder and ignitor were in her pack, which would have been collected as evidence by now. She needed something else. Something fast and effective that couldn't be traced back to her.

She left her building and bought moonshine from a street

vendor. Soon she was pushing her way through the brush of a long overgrown urban park, following the subtle trail of broken branches and an occasional bit of litter until she found what she was looking for—an assortment of shin-high stumps encircling a rusted metal ring and the remnants of charred wood.

She'd been out here once before, the scene of a campfire party that turned out to be mostly teenagers seizing an opportunity to grope at each other, fueled by the dim light and cheap alcohol. Ainsley had stayed no more than five minutes but she was glad, in retrospect, to have learned about this spot. There was little risk of anyone showing up before midday, and a fire in the pit wouldn't alarm anyone if they did.

Ainsley emptied her incriminating clothes and an armful of dry wood scraps into the pit before dousing it with the cheap moonshine. Unsure of how flammable it would be, she lit the tip of a broken branch and tossed it from several paces away. A blue flame raced across the material and soon a tapestry of colors danced in the fire pit.

The irony was not lost on Ainsley as she waited for fire to consume the clothes she'd worn while fleeing the site of a fiery explosion.

She fed the pit with more detritus until there was no evidence of the fabric. Then she poured out the remaining moonshine and muttered a goodbye to Jasmine before wiping the bottle free of her fingerprints and tossing it into the surrounding woods, where she guessed it would be one of many discarded liquor containers.

On the way home, she stopped at Ross Sundries and Supplies for water, soap, and a box of food rations. It wasn't the most appetizing way to stay fed, but the supply would see her through the next several days without more trips out.

While the gray-haired store owner tapped the prices into an oversized tablet, Ainsley thumbed through a yellowing stack of cruise brochures.

"You interested in a cruise, kid? I can sell you a cruise. A few nights out on Lake Ontario? You'd love it. You know what they say: cruises are the crack cocaine of vacations."

"The crack what?"

"Crack cocaine. You never heard of crack cocaine?"

Ainsley shook her head and he frowned.

"You sure you aren't interested in a cruise? Hard to beat a cruise. I went on one once. Glorious. Most food I've ever seen. Not cheap, mind you. But you know what they say, it could've been cheaper but it wouldn't have been as much fun."

"I'm good. Thanks."

"Your loss, kid."

He read out her total—the same amount Ainsley had already calculated in her head—and she pressed an anonymous currency token against his tablet to transfer the funds.

Lost in thought on the walk home, she nearly tripped over one of the neighborhood's stray dogs. Pet ownership had gone out of style when Ainsley was a young girl. She remembered wanting a dog and being heartbroken when her parents told her it was inhumane.

Even so, the feral dogs in her neighborhood had names given to them by the local children. They'd named all of the strays, though Ainsley didn't know which name belonged to this particular dog.

It gazed at her with expectant eyes. It was beyond malnourished. Every rib was visible under a thin coat of dirty, matted fur. Dogs that hadn't been caught and eaten in more desperate neighborhoods had mostly followed old instincts and roamed in packs like their ancestors. This one, for whatever reason, seemed intent on holding on to companionship with humans, behavior that had been bred in for centuries but no longer held much advantage.

The thing was too gaunt and pathetic for Ainsley to ignore, so she tore open a ration bar and tossed a chunk. The dog snatched it greedily and made a whimpering sound when it saw that she wasn't going to toss more.

"You should learn to hunt rats. No shortage of them around."

Back in her room, Ainsley's stomach rumbled and complained as she washed down mouthfuls of ration bar with water. She couldn't deny that she'd let things go too far the night before.

She stretched out on the cot and listened to the murmuring of her digestive system while she pondered Miriam's offer. Taking the job was foolish. She knew that. Even if Miriam had been convincing and charismatic. Ainsley was going to have to be absolutely convinced that she was making the right decision in order for her resolve to hold when the woman came for an answer.

It was still early when the lights turned off from the lack of movement in the room. With no windows to let in natural light, Ainsley soon found herself yawning, and she let sleep take her.

It was dark when she started to rouse. Ainsley let her hand

drop over the edge of the bed to the floor and found her bracelet computer with her fingers. She croaked out a request for the time.

"8:39am," the computer replied.

"You sure?" Ainsley mumbled. "I thought I set the wake program for eight. Lights on."

Nothing happened.

"Lights on," she repeated.

Still nothing.

She sat up and rubbed a palm against one eye, a habit she'd had since she was a little girl. She blinked several times, not fully awake, and wondered why the room wasn't pitch black if the lights were out.

The glow of a handheld tablet computer illuminated the face of a man sitting in her folding chair. He had one leg slung over the other casually. For a moment, Ainsley thought she was dreaming, but the man spoke when he saw her moving.

"About time you woke up. Who sleeps this late on a work day?"

"You're in the wrong room, guy."

"No, I'm here for you."

Ainsley pressed the bracelet computer again. "Computer, code porcupine."

"That's not going to work."

"Computer, code porcupine. Acknowledge."

The computer beeped. "That function is not available at this time."

The man tapped at his tablet computer and its light went out. Ainsley shoved her hand under her pillow, feeling around for the small stun baton she kept there. She hadn't found it when the room lights snapped on a moment later.

She squinted against the sudden brilliance.

"Looking for this?"

Through a swirl of fading stars, she saw her stun baton in his hand and the air felt like it cooled several degrees. Ainsley began doing a mental inventory of the things in her room. There was precious little she could use as a weapon. The near-empty water jug was too unwieldy. Was she going to bludgeon him with food ration bars?

The man hadn't moved from the chair and Ainsley wondered if there was still a chance she could talk her way out of this.

"So, what can I do for you?" she asked, forcing a casualness into her voice that she didn't feel.

"Miriam asked me to come collect your answer for her."

"Miriam?"

"Yeah, tall lady, nice apartment. Saved your ass after you drank yourself into a stupor."

"I know who she is. I thought she was going to come herself."

"She sent me instead."

"Why? Does she think a man is going to intimidate me into saying yes?"

He laughed. "If that worked, you wouldn't be much use to us. She's busy with other preparations. I'm here because she thinks you'll say no."

"I see. I should say no, shouldn't I? The whole thing sounds grandiose and risky, and I don't know you people."

He shrugged. "Depends on your point of view. I've done seven jobs with this crew. They're a good bunch. Besides, you didn't know your last partner when you started working with her, did you? But you figured out how to trust her. Sorry about your loss, by the way. It hurts to lose good people."

Ainsley nodded at the condolence. This guy was right—she hadn't known Jasmine at first. But they'd started small. Miriam and her messenger boy weren't proposing to start small.

"What if I hear the details and then decide I want out?"

"That would be fine. We work from a safe house. You'll be required to stay isolated in the house until the op is complete. We'd keep you fed and give you some books to read or something."

"That sounds suspiciously magnanimous."

"We're not monsters. We're businesspeople. Bringing you on is an investment. There's a calculated risk, but it's a bigger risk to not have the right person for the role. And Miriam is convinced you're the right person."

"But you aren't?"

"I think you've got potential but this is bigger than anything you've pulled before."

Ainsley watched his body language, trying to decide if he was manipulating her. It was an obvious technique to tear her down a little so her ego would want her to prove herself. Or it could be a genuine concern.

Manipulation or not, Ainsley wanted to know more.

"Alright, I'm in. For now."

So much for my resolve.

"Excellent." The man stood and extended his arm, palm facing her. "I'm Eddie, by the way."

Her sleepwear was minimal and she wasn't in the habit of parading herself in front of strange men, but she felt that taking the time to wrap herself in a blanket would project a false sense of weakness, so she stood and pressed her palm against his. Eddie's eyes glanced down, but to his credit, they didn't linger. If nothing else, it was prudent of him to check for a weapon. As he'd said, trust took time.

He did, however, stumble over his words a little. "I'll, uh, give you a minute to get ready. And gather up anything personal or perishable. It'll be a while before you come back here."

He stepped out of the room and Ainsley dressed, opting for tear-resistant fabrics and plenty of pockets.

The only meaningful thing she owned was a pewter ornament of two doves on a piece of red ribbon. It had been a gift from Raita the Christmas before last when the little girl learned that Ainsley—or Esther as the girl knew her—owned no Christmas decorations. She couldn't bring herself to tell the girl that she wasn't at all religious and that even if she was, her family was Jewish. Ainsley dropped the decoration in a pocket. If she never made it back to this room, at least Raita wouldn't find the trinket abandoned. Ainsley knew how it felt to be disappointed by grownups. She didn't want to be that type of adult. Besides, it would be nice to have something small to remind her of home.

She stuffed extra clothes into her laundry bag, leaving behind the dressier items she wore to her day job as the human failsafe in an automated equipment rental store. Her parents would be furious when they learned that she'd stopped showing up for work. Her father had pulled strings to arrange the stable but tedious job. It would be one more mark supporting their supposition that she was drifting through life. Ainsley didn't care much about their opinions but that didn't mean she would enjoy suffering the inevitable lecture. They were still her parents.

When she joined Eddie in the hallway, he looked at the mostly empty laundry bag.

"That's all you're bringing?"

"I don't own much more than this."

"The job'll be weeks at least. Could be a couple months."

"Oh, should I pack a formal gown then?"

She held a deadpan expression until Eddie laughed and slapped her on the arm. "I may end up liking you after all. So nothing you're forgetting? You won't be asking me to bring you back for something in two days?"

"No, this will do."

"Then let's get going. There's a laundromat about three blocks north of here. You know the one?"

Ainsley nodded that she did.

"Meet me there in fifteen minutes. I'll pull up in a blue car with tinted windows. Get in and we'll be on our way. Do both of us a favor and don't talk to anybody. Don't draw attention to yourself, and, most importantly, when you get to the laundromat, put your bracelet in this bag and throw it in a washing machine. Run the machine on heavy duty cycle."

Eddie passed her a translucent yellow bag filled with fine powder, a half-liter worth or more.

"You're serious?"

"One hundred percent. Too many signals coming and going from a consumer-grade wrist computer. We'll have something better for you to use. Once the bag gets saturated, the chemical inside will dissolve most of the material that your bracelet is made from."

Fifteen minutes later, Ainsley climbed into the car. The windows around her turned fully opaque as it pulled away.

CHAPTER 6

EDDIE SAT IN the front, consumed by something on his tablet computer while the car drove itself.

Ainsley asked, "Do you know where we're going?"

"To the safe house."

"I mean, do you know where the safe house is? Since the windows are all shaded, I can't tell where we're going."

"Yes, I know where the safe house is. It's too early for us to tell you that. I'm sure you understand."

He returned his attention to his tablet and they drove in silence. Either Eddie wasn't one for small talk or he'd yet to decide if it was worth his time to talk with her.

She scraped a bit of grime from under a fingernail, maintaining a relaxed posture and refusing to show her agitation. Even though they had come to her, her new employers were being very cautious. Or were they partners? She didn't know enough yet to even decide how to think of them.

Without her bracelet computer or visual cues from outside, Ainsley found it hard to estimate how far they'd traveled. It felt like they were in transit for close to an hour, which could put them in any far-flung corner of the old Toronto sprawl. The roads they drove over were rough, but that was typical almost everywhere in the city.

When the car finally stopped, the windows faded to semi-transparent to reveal the inside of a concrete garage. Ainsley's door opened. Holding it was a man who had to be at least 270 pounds of nothing but muscle.

"This is Francis," Eddie said as he came around the car. "Our head of security."

"Head of security? I *am* security, mate." To Ainsley, he said, "Need to check you over for trackers, transmitters, weapons, implanted devices, you know the drill."

Ainsley nodded, although she did not know the drill. He patted her down first and then checked the contents of her laundry tote. Next came a wand that clicked and whirred as he waved it around her body and bag.

When he was done with the wand, he placed a hoop on the floor, four or five feet across, and asked her to step in the middle of it. He lifted it slowly until it was over her head. He consulted his tablet for a moment then repeated the procedure with her bag.

Finally, he guided her into a tall box and closed the door. The machine emitted a red light that gave the tiny space an eerie feel. The box popped and an electronic voice told her the scan was complete.

"All clear," Francis said.

"What was all that?"

"Standard protocol. Metal detector, scans for electronics, radiation, and other signals. The box is a general disinfectant. Ultraviolet light, bit of radiation, basically a micro EMP just in case the scanners missed anything. Corporate security level stuff. Not military grade. Good enough for our safe house."

"Radiation and an EMP? Did you nuke me without my consent?"

"We didn't nuke you." Francis held his fingers in air quotes when he said nuke. "It's a common procedure, perfectly safe."

Ainsley felt like her skin was crawling. "Give a girl a little notice next time, would you?"

Not only did Francis not grin, his expression didn't change at all.

Maybe his muscles squeezed out his sense of humor...

Eddie tapped Ainsley on her left shoulder blade. "Come on, let's go chat with Miriam."

In contrast to the sparse garage, the house showed evidence of considerable activity. Several desks and tables held boxes, tablets, and enough display screens to be a real ops center.

There were physical file folders on some of the desks. Ainsley had seen lots of paper in her life, but it was far from common because the Qyntarak imposed hefty levies on tree harvesting.

"More trees, fewer people. Better for the planet," her father had said to her growing up. It was one of countless mantras repeated by collaborators.

Ainsley stole glances at the handwritten labels.

Schedules.

Station personnel.

Terrain and geography.

"Oh, Ainsley, good, you came. Come join me. I just made fresh tea."

From the far side of the room, Miriam waved her hand in a beckoning motion and Ainsley obliged the request.

A thin column of steam swirled from the spout of a teapot. It reminded Ainsley of something her grandmother had owned years ago. It was ornate and looked delicate, out of place amongst the desks and electronics.

"Sit, sit." Miriam gestured to the empty chair across from her.

Eddie sat next to Ainsley. Francis hung back several steps, his arms folded across his chest and his expression on the grim side of neutral.

Miriam filled two teacups and offered one to Eddie, who dismissed it with a subtle wave.

"Eddie doesn't see the point of the ritual of a good pot of tea." The teacup and saucer clinked as Miriam set them in front of Ainsley. "It's only whiskey, water, or caffeine pills with this one. Appallingly utilitarian, if you ask me."

Miriam winked at Eddie.

He crossed one leg over the other and wrapped his fingers together behind his head so that his elbows stuck out. "You let me know when that stops working out for you."

She smiled at him then asked Ainsley, "Do you take anything in your tea? I have some sugar and a little milk powder."

"Real milk powder? From cow's milk?"

"Of course, a small supply. It is fantastically difficult to acquire these days, as I'm certain you can appreciate."

"I can't say I've had much opportunity to acquire a taste for it. A swirl of honey would be good enough for me."

"Honey we have in ample quantities. Francis, would you mind fetching some for our new teammate?"

From behind her, Ainsley heard Francis grunt. She couldn't be certain but she didn't think it sounded like a friendly, happy-to-help grunt.

"If I'm honest, I don't much care for the milk powder myself. I keep it for the prestige of it. Because I can."

Francis returned quickly and everyone watched while Ainsley prepared her tea. The experience was surreal and made her anxious to move on to the bigger topics that everyone was surely waiting for.

"Let's get started then, shall we?" Miriam spoke with a smile then sipped from her teacup. "I must admit that I didn't think I had you convinced. I'm so glad you're here. We have all the pieces in place to move forward with our operation, which is wonderful."

"I'm here tentatively. Until I learn more about the job."

"How familiar are you with exile and red ships?"

"I know that the Qyntarak forced hundreds of thousands of humans onto ships and exiled them into high orbit a couple decades ago. And they condemn more people all the time to be slaves on red ships."

"Millions of people in those first exiles, actually," Miriam said. "But I'm not asking about the history of them. Are you familiar with how they operate?"

"I know that people who accumulate debt are sent up—"

"She doesn't know," Eddie said. "Obviously."

His interjection annoyed her but he was right. Ainsley didn't know how the ships operated, only that she hated the

Qyntarak for controlling the planet, forcing humans to live in cramped spaceships, and disguising slavery as debt repayment.

"Fair enough," Miriam said. "Not many people really understand how they operate. That's fine, I didn't want to presume, given your parents…"

"I'd rather not discuss my parents, if it's all the same to you."

"At some point, that might be necessary, but we can leave it for now. The exile ships, as you've said, are in a very high orbit around the Earth. The red ships, or service ships as they're more properly known, are companions to larger Qyntarak starships. Each Qyntarak ship has many service ships assigned to it to house the humans who serve the Qyntarak. All of those ships require supplies. Although they are efficient, they aren't closed systems.

"Fresh and dehydrated food are the most common things sent up from the planet. Shipments go up all the time. Some in automated pods, some in larger shuttles with a human crew. And, of course, there's a thriving black market. Bribes, corruption, and grift are as old as shipping and commerce itself. Tea and coffee, for example, are often smuggled as gifts for family members. I've heard they're even a form of currency up there."

Ainsley had started chewing on her lip, concerned about the direction the conversation had taken. "Please tell me you aren't planning to steal food and supplies meant for people trapped on those ships."

Miriam laughed at her again. "Goodness, no. We aren't devils."

"So you're smuggling something then?"

"No," Miriam said, "we are planning to take something."

Eddie uncrossed his leg and leaned forward in his seat. "Most of the shipments that go up are consumables like food. Even if we were willing to steal that, the payoff wouldn't be worth the risk. But every so often, a shipment is something else, something worth the risk. That's what we're going after. The big Qyntarak starships are designed to fly across star systems. They have gravity manipulation technology and massive energy reserves to power their ships for years."

"Decades, in some cases," Miriam added.

Eddie's voice got a little louder and a little faster. "But just like human tech, the Qyntarak's wears out and breaks. One of the ships up there is gearing up for some big repair work. They're going to be moving a huge shipment in a few weeks. Energy cells, gravity control components, and things we don't even understand. We're going to take it all."

"You want to steal a bunch of alien technology?" Ainsley said. "And then what? You won't be able to use it or sell it. You'd risk blowing a hole in the side of the planet if you tried to destroy it."

Miriam downed the rest of her tea and returned the cup to its saucer with a soft clink. "I'm afraid I'm not at liberty to read you in on the broader mission, but rest assured that we have a patron with a plan and resources."

"A patron? Hold on, you didn't mention that before."

"I'm mentioning it now. Ainsley, we are not some ragtag band of anarchists poking a giant with sticks. Our patron sponsors the upfront costs, provides intelligence data, and worries about what happens to the goods once we've acquired them. We work for our patron."

"When do I meet this patron?"

"You don't. Look, you're used to calling your own shots. We understand. This won't be like that. It can't. I didn't have to tell you that our job was sponsored by a patron. I chose to because I believe trust and transparency will make us a stronger team. All I'm asking for is trust in return. I promise I will tell you the things you need to know."

The memory of Jasmine sticking a pop box to the fuel tank flashed through her mind...

Trust... The things she needed to know... Loyalty....
Teammates... Her parents....

Little Raita.... An exploding tentacle.... The smell of clothes being consumed by flames...

The smell of ape meat on a platter... Her mother in a breathing mask placing it before a Qyntarak scientist....

"Hey. Yo, kid." Eddie snapped his fingers in front of her face.

"I'm—I'm sorry," she stammered. "I was thinking."

"Do we have an understanding?" Miriam asked.

"Yes. I can agree to that. What exactly do you need me to do?"

CHAPTER 7

THE BUS LURCHED just enough to make the bodies inside sway. A worker reached for a handhold and the smell from his armpit made Ben wrinkle his nose. The guy was rank for the start of a shift. Ben didn't know him but guessed he must work two jobs. Plenty of people did that to make ends meet. If he was general labor at the warehouse, he'd barely make enough to feed himself.

"You'd think those six-armed hermies could spring for a grav stabilizer in the shuttle bus, no?" The foul-smelling worker was talking to no one and everyone at once, but he was looking at Ben when he said it.

"It's half a kilometer from the entrance to the staging warehouse. We're lucky they provide a shuttle at all. And they aren't hermaphrodites."

The man looked at Ben with confusion. "Sure they are. They're all both boys and girls. Everyone knows that."

"No, their species doesn't have sexes. They don't reproduce like anything on Earth."

"What are you, their nacking PR person?"

"I'm just a guy who works here." Ben stretched out an arm to grab his own handhold. "And I don't want to see a colleague sent off planet because he said something ignorant in front of the wrong cantankerous alien."

The change in the worker's expression told Ben that raising his arm had opened his jacket enough for the other man to see the red of his supervisor's badge.

The bus jerked to a stop and the mass of people on board began shifting toward the exits. Ben didn't notice Kamil until he was two feet away with a conspiratorial smile on his face.

"Throwing your weight around, I see."

At six feet eight inches tall and over 300 pounds the last time anyone had bothered to check, Ben was the biggest person in most rooms. He only felt small during the occasional inspections by visiting Qyntarak. But he knew that wasn't what Kamil meant.

"Better a human supervisor than one of them. If a Qyntarak's here, they're not in a good mood to start with."

"I'm still having trouble coming to grips with them making you a shift supervisor."

"The way I heard it, you were up for the spot but everyone said you were too ugly for the job. Figured you'd scare off trainees on their first day."

"You're management now. I think that's harassment."

"Sometimes the truth hurts. I'm just honest to a fault."

They grew quiet as they joined the queue for their second security check of the morning. There was no policy forbidding conversation at the security checkpoints but it had been that way for all the years he'd worked there.

The crowd spread out once past the bottleneck of the scanners and the glassy stares of the two humans charged with monitoring the hundreds of workers streaming in and out each day.

"Speaking of truth," Kamil said, "what happened with that last report about your wife?"

Ben could tell that he was frowning before he could will his face to stay neutral. "Request denied. Doesn't seem to matter what angle I take, it's always a closed door."

"Unbelievable. A whole neighborhood just whisked away with no explanation. I don't know how we ever let things like that happen."

"Read a bit of history. Humans were doing—" Chirping from his wrist computer cut Ben off. "Ah, crap. I need to go back. Forgot that I have a trainee starting today."

"Your first chance to teach some fresh meat to do things the right way for a change." Kamil gave him a mock salute. "Make us proud, captain."

Ben gave an exaggerated roll of his eyes and went back through the security checkpoint to where his trainee stood alone only a few feet from where the bus had dropped her off.

"Ainsley?"

She waved. "That's me. Are you Mr. Triggs?"

"Please, call me Ben."

He extended his palm and she pressed hers against his in greeting.

"You ever work as a cargo management specialist before?"

Ainsley shook her head no. "First time. I'm looking forward to learning."

"Well, it's hard work and the pay is lousy, but it's a good honest job. Important too. A lot of people up there depend on us getting the necessities of life to them on schedule."

"You make it sound almost noble."

"I think it is." He slapped his hands together. "Let's get you through security and settled in. You've got a long day ahead of you."

Ben gestured and talked as they made their way toward his office. "This is a staging warehouse. That means we accept delivery of shipments of cargo, most of which are destined to be sent into orbit. Things come in by delivery truck or grav train. We store and organize the cargo here and when it's time for a launch, we look after loading it onto delivery shuttles or automated pods. Sometimes, depending on the delivery, a couple of us go up on the shuttle to facilitate."

Ben stopped in front of an RV-4 unit.

"That's a powered exoskeleton suit. This job involves moving a lot of stuff around so we use machinery like the suits or those remote controlled manipulating arms over there to help out. No sense in ruining a perfectly good back when there's gear to make the job faster and safer. Alright, let's—"

Ben paused as he thought about Ainsley's day of reading regulations and his own day. The mountain of administrative work could wait a few extra minutes.

"How about you try your hand at a practice run in the RV-4 here? You'll need to get certified before you can use it on the job but maybe get a taste of what you can look forward to? What do you think?"

Ainsley gave him an enthusiastic smile. It was one of

those smiles that used her entire face, and he could see in her eyes that it was genuine. He had a good feeling about his first trainee.

"Sounds like fun."

Ben helped her get situated in the exoskeleton and walked her through the basics of making it step forward, reach down, and pick up a box from the floor. She missed the box several times then batted it around the floor until she eventually secured it between the oversized hands of the suit.

When he applauded, it seemed to startle her and she relaxed her grip, dropping the box to the floor with a thud.

"I'm so sorry."

Ben shrugged. "Don't worry about it. That's why we have training and certifications. Anyone here tells you that they didn't drop something on their first day in an exoskeleton is a dirty liar. You'll get better with practice, I promise."

He coached her through returning the exoskeleton to its charging cradle.

"Alright, come on," he said once she'd extricated herself from the suit. "I'll buy you a coffee and get you set up on the computer system so you can do your training and learn how we juggle the schedules."

CHAPTER 8

THE WINDOWS OF the driverless car were shaded again as it returned Ainsley to the safe house. She turned off the interior lights, hoping for a short nap before her first debrief meeting.

Inside the house, Miriam sat with perfect posture in an elegant old chair. Three more chairs sat unoccupied around a low circular table on which a tea service was arranged. Ainsley noted three teacups.

"Good morning. I trust your ride was uneventful."

"Uneventful, if you don't count being driven to an unknown destination to engage in scheming and conspiracies."

Miriam didn't laugh but the comment seemed to amuse her. She patted the armrest of the chair to her left. "Please sit. This is your home for the duration of our time together. There's no need for you to stand like a guest."

If Ainsley had to place a wager, she would put Miriam in her late thirties, but she had an air about her that made her seem older and unambiguously in charge of the room. It was a compelling trick.

Miriam reached across the gap between the chairs and placed a hand on Ainsley's forearm in an almost motherly way. "So, tell me, how was your first night at the warehouse?"

"Tedious. Exhausting. How can it be so tiring to sit in front of a screen for hours just reading? Do you want to hear the load capacity of one arm of an RV-4 exoskeleton suit?"

This time Miriam smiled. "Not right this minute. But I know someone who will be interested in that. The others will be along in just a moment. Tea?"

Ainsley nodded and Miriam poured. By the time she had finished filling all three teacups, Eddie and another woman had entered the room.

"Good, the gang's all here. Ainsley, I'd like you to meet the final member of our little crew. This is Wanda."

The woman pushed past Eddie and raised her palm in greeting. Ainsley's gaze flitted from the woman's face to her outstretched hand, then to her feet, and back to her face. Ainsley neither flinched nor gasped, but her mind was racing in an attempt to determine what might have disfigured the woman.

Her face and neck looked as if they had been mangled and left to heal without medical attention. Her hand had deep grooves and scar tissue running from her pinky finger to the base of her thumb like rows of a grotesque pink garden. She moved with a slight limp and Ainsley thought, at a glance, that her shoes might be different sizes.

Ainsley realized that she was taking too long to respond and popped up from her seat awkwardly, extending her own palm and almost stumbling as she pressed it against Wanda's.

"Nice to meet you."

"No need to get up on my behalf." Wanda dropped into the empty seat across from Miriam. Eddie took the final seat opposite Ainsley.

"I took the liberty of pouring you tea." Miriam slid a cup across the table. "Wanda is our technology expert. She'll want to hear about what you've seen and learned so far after your first shift."

"What do you want to know?"

Wanda picked up her teacup and blew on the steaming liquid. "All of it. I'll ask if we need you to go into more detail on anything."

Ainsley raised her own cup and took a careful test sip, buying herself a moment to collect her thoughts.

"My supervisor is a man named Benjamin Triggs. He's casual. Goes by Ben. Doesn't like being called Mr. Triggs. Friendly. Personable. He was a few minutes late meeting me. I suspect he went through the security checkpoint and had to come back, possibly because he forgot I was coming."

Wanda raised a finger to stop Ainsley. "And the inner security checkpoint? Automated scanners and human backups?"

"Yes. Two humans. And an interesting tidbit about the checkpoint—nobody talks in line while waiting."

"Is that a rule? Or just convention?"

"It didn't occur to me to ask."

"Always ask questions." Miriam shifted so she was leaning

forward in her chair. "You need to be incredibly inquisitive. Not just because we need all the information we can get but because asking about everything will make it less conspicuous when you ask about things that we absolutely must know. Asking questions must be an essential part of your persona."

Ainsley nodded. Miriam was right and Ainsley was embarrassed that she hadn't thought of it in those terms. Fortunately, it was still easy to evolve her persona. No one expected a new employee to be herself in the beginning. Everyone had nerves on their first day.

"What brand and model were the security scanners?"

"I don't recall. I'm sure I saw the Aldebaran logo, but I didn't notice a model number."

Wanda tapped on a tablet computer for several seconds then spun it around and handed it to Ainsley.

"Was it one of these?"

Ainsley swiped through the pictures on the tablet. She'd been busy studying the people around her, especially Ben, and had paid little attention to the scanners.

"The ASC-8701 or maybe the ASC-9200. Pretty sure it's one of those."

"Pretty sure?" There was irritation in Wanda's voice now. "You're pretty sure? I'm one hundred percent sure that pretty sure is what gets people caught. Or worse. An ASC-9200 can do multi-part component conjecture across a 200 scan sliding window. Meanwhile, the 8701 has a known factory defect that causes false positives on irregularly shaped ceramic insulators, unless you have the patched 8701a version."

Ainsley stared dumbstruck at Wanda. The positive feeling

about her first day evaporated.

Wanda's eyes shifted to Miriam.

"Are we training interns now? Did somebody forget to send me the memo? We can't make solid plans if we don't have solid data. Sloppy and irresponsible reconnaissance data will tank an otherwise solid mission."

The four of them sat in tense silence for several long seconds.

"Are you quite done?" Miriam asked.

"I think the better question is whether we're all done. Not sure about anyone else, but I'm not super keen on mopping up Qyntarak slobber on some red ship because our person on the ground can't tell the difference between the 8701 and the 9200."

Miriam returned her teacup to the table with a little more force than was prudent for fine china.

"Thank you, Wanda. Your concerns are noted. I trust that all of us can work together to coach our newest team member on what we expect from her for her part of the mission. It does us no good to complain and criticize instead of encouraging and cooperating with each other. Is that clear?"

It took several more seconds but everyone nodded in agreement. Ainsley filled in the rest of the details of her shift. Wanda was at least a little appeased that she'd remembered the model number of the exoskeleton suit. She was also pleased to learn that Ainsley already had access to the computer system. Wanda walked her through a list of things she needed to know about the computers so she could configure a smart virus that would burrow its way in and grant them remote access.

Once Miriam was satisfied with her debrief and Ainsley had demonstrated that she'd memorized the items on Wanda's list, they dismissed her to her room so she could sleep before her next shift.

CHAPTER 9

AINSLEY STARED INTO her own eyes. Her reflection was distorted by the hazy antique mirror. The safe house had eight bedrooms and five bathrooms. No one even had to share. It was a new luxury for Ainsley. Before the chaos of the last century, her city had been affluent to the point that such things were common, but she scarcely believed some of the stories. And that was ancient history. She'd only ever known a world under the control of the Qyntarak—a world in which few humans were allowed to direct their own lives.

Her father used to say that humans had squandered their chance to look after the planet. He told anyone who would listen to him that the Qyntarak had saved humanity. They had been a disease that evolved into something that was killing its own host, and the Qyntarak were doctors cutting out the infection.

Ainsley had never cared for that metaphor. She resented

him comparing his own species to a parasitic disease. But disapproving of her father's opinions and actions was old territory that she didn't need to revisit. She just wanted the alien stranglehold to loosen. No, what she truly wanted was for the Qyntarak to leave.

That, in theory, was what Miriam was offering her. It wasn't a direct path to driving away the Qyntarak, but they were building on something bigger that was going to lessen their influence.

She had to do this thing for Miriam.

She must do her part.

She would push past her guilt about manipulating innocents at the warehouse.

When the job was done and Ainsley disappeared, questions would be asked. Suspicious eyes would look at her supervisor and her coworkers. But Miriam and Eddie were steadfast in their conviction that there would be no serious consequences for humans in the aftermath. Someone like Ben Triggs might get a demotion. Worst case, they fired a few people. People got fired all the time. It was unlikely that they would send anyone to a red ship because an unknown group ripped off a train on its way to the warehouse.

According to Eddie, the grav trains were fully automated so there would be no people on board. It really was a straightforward plan without repercussions for humans.

After Miriam's revelation that the Qyntarak could no longer be evaded with facial deformers, there was no going back to the way she used to operate. Once this job was finished, her own face would put Ainsley at risk every time she went out in public. Anywhere the Qyntarak hooked into video feeds, they might find her. So she had to make this job count. She got one swing of the sword and she needed to draw blood.

The face staring back at her in the mirror was resolute.

She turned the tap handle to let a trickle of warm water run into the sink. She cupped her hands and let them fill slowly before splashing it across her face. Looking at her reflected self one more time, she whispered, "Goodbye, Esther."

CHAPTER 10

AINSLEY SPENT THE next eight nights reporting every tidbit of intelligence she could extract from the warehouse back to Wanda. Like most Qyntarak-controlled facilities, warehouse shifts ran nine days on and three days off. There were rumors that the Qyntarak preferred systems based on multiples of three because they had three tentacles on each side of their bodies, much like humans had a tendency to use fives and tens because they had five fingers on each hand, but it was only speculation. The Qyntarak had never been forthcoming about their home world, their culture, or their history. Everything humans knew had been pieced together from fragments of information passed on by word of mouth.

Ainsley squeezed her eyes shut tighter in a futile effort to quiet her thoughts and get some sleep. Her transition to working nights was harder than she'd expected. She was exhausted and irritable.

Miriam had given her permission to relax on the first of her three days off. She slept on and off through the day until Francis invited her to eat with the team. It surprised her to learn that their stern-looking security chief was also an avid cook who made meals that rivaled anything she'd ever eaten.

Over dinner, Eddie shared that he had a lead on a cargo hauler. "An acquaintance of an acquaintance deals in off-the-books acquisition of the kind of equipment we need. He has a couple that are powerful enough to tow the grav train cars once we detach them."

"Wonderful news," Miriam said. "We're cutting it close on that rather essential part of the plan."

"It's my number one priority right now. I need to go test out the options tomorrow. I'd like to take Ainsley with me. Pose as vertical farm entrepreneurs looking to move planting beds and crops. That'll give us a cover story for needing stable hover and heavy towing. We can say we're trying to cut out the middleman to do our own deliveries."

"Why me?" It made no sense to Ainsley. She wasn't sure Eddie liked her, never mind trusted her.

He had a pained expression on his face and didn't answer. After an extended silence, Wanda said, "My face is too memorable for ops in public. Miriam and Francis are hard to believe as farmers."

It was the first time anyone had referenced Wanda's scars. Ainsley was embarrassed for having drawn it out, even if it was unintentional. She looked at Francis's massive arms stretching his shirt sleeves taut. She decided to take a chance on diffusing the awkwardness with humor.

"Well, if Francis here wasn't so scrawny. Do you even work out?"

His forkful of casserole stopped in midair. "Two hours every day. You've seen me in the gym downstairs."

Ainsley relaxed a little as grins spread around the table.

THE FOLLOWING AFTERNOON, Eddie familiarized himself with the controls of the cargo hauler while Ainsley adjusted her seat.

"Obviously, the last co-pilot was a tad bigger than me."

The wiry salesman with his slicked back hair hovered behind them in the cramped cockpit. "This thing was repossessed from a construction contractor. The crew would've worn gear and harnesses. They'd be floating up and down, getting in and out all the time. Don't worry, though, these seats will fit anyone once you get them set right."

He leaned in and slid a hand over her lower ribs while tugging on a strap with his other hand. Ainsley brought her elbow down to push his groping hand away.

"I'm fine."

He pulled his hands back and feigned contrition.

"What do you think there, sport?" he asked Eddie. "Meets your needs right well, I'd say. I told you it would, didn't I?"

"I'll need to take it up and put it through its paces."

"Sure, sure, that's great. Let me strap in and we can take her up."

"We can take it up ourselves," Ainsley said.

"Oh, little miss, no offense but this here is an expensive piece of equipment. I can't let you take her out unaccompanied."

"You have our car as collateral," Eddie said. "And you have a tracker and remote kill switch installed on this thing, right? We'll go up the two of us."

The salesman didn't respond immediately but forced the smile back on his face. "Whatever you say, sport. Customer's always right, am I right?"

Eddie waited for the man to disembark and give them a thumbs up from outside. Eddie waved and turned his attention back to the controls.

The pilot's console of the old hauler was a combination of oversized physical buttons and switches designed to be used while wearing gloves. Eddie toggled several and the machine hummed to life.

"Computer, take off and hover at fifty feet."

The machine lurched upward and Ainsley's stomach danced with the sudden movement. A moment later, a computerized voice said, "Hovering at fifty feet."

"Voice control in an industrial machine?"

"Limited. These old buckets are a mishmash of interfaces. This one would've been designed to allow full AI control, too, from before the Qyntarak clamped down on humans owning AIs. Once Wanda removes the governor module, it'll be able to do lots on its own."

"So you think this is good for the job?"

"It's old but well maintained. Only way to know for sure is to stretch its legs. Hold on."

Eddie stomped on a pair of floor pedals while pulling back and turning the steering handle, sending the hauler up and to the left with a jolt that made Ainsley's harness bite into her shoulder.

Eddie let out a whoop as the hauler banked and rose. "It's got some kick when it's not towing anything."

Ainsley looked out the window and watched the buildings shrink away. She had flown countless times but never in something so utilitarian. It wasn't uncomfortable, but everything from the controls and seats to the stark gray color scheme and aggressive handling made it clear that the ship was designed for work and not leisure.

"Wanda and Francis have a scanning gate set up outside the city. We'll fly there and give it a scan. They'll let us know if there's anything unseen that we need to worry about."

"How did you know back there that it had a tracker installed?"

"An educated guess. Places like that sell to sketchy customers. No matter what he tells us about where this thing came from, it's been through a bunch of owners already. Probably been repossessed a couple times. They put a tracker and a kill switch on it, sell to someone who can't really afford it, and take it back five minutes after they miss their first payment."

"Always good to see humanity sticking together."

Eddie shrugged his shoulders without taking his hand off the steering column. "Everyone's just trying to survive. Not sure it's fair to fault him for that."

"Humans survived in the first place because we learned how to communicate and trust each other. Humans were never the strongest or the fastest, but we became the dominant species. So, yeah, I can blame them a little bit. If everyone thinks about themselves, we're a lost cause."

"When you put it like that, it sounds like the Qyntarak should be in charge. They communicate and cooperate with each other. They're bigger, faster, got better tech. And if you believe their propaganda, we were well on our way to wiping ourselves off our own planet anyway. Like 'em or hate 'em, they did help us figure a few things out."

Ainsley couldn't tell if he was goading her or making casual conversation. Whatever his intention, Eddie was pushing her buttons and she could feel the tingle of her fight-or-flight response prodding her to argue. She'd suppress those feelings if it wasn't just the two of them. Understanding each other's point of view didn't feel like a bad idea. Another way to build trust and all that.

"You're such a fan of what they've done for our planet, why in the world would you be working against them?"

"You're kidding, right? If someone comes into your home, you need to defend it. Those alien assholes have been walking around like they own the place for too long. Also, the money's pretty good."

Ainsley felt her muscles start to relax. "You were starting to worry me there for a minute. You sounded like my father."

Eddie's head swiveled in her direction and then back to the windshield. Ainsley pretended to study the glowing lights of a touchscreen in front of her. She'd opened up enough. She wasn't going to talk about her parents, and she hoped that Eddie would have the decency to let her comment stand on its own.

He didn't. "Your father runs one of the human-Qyntarak liaison offices, doesn't he?"

He phrased it as a question but if he knew to ask, he already knew the answer.

Without looking up, she said, "That's right."

"The apple fell pretty far from the tree."

"I'm not really into selling out my species for personal gain."

"He's a true believer?"

"I think a lot of people can be convinced that they believe

something if you give them a big enough house and a full enough plate."

"Sounds like someone's got daddy issues," he said with a laugh.

Ainsley gave him a contemptuous scowl. "Look, I'm sure you're just trying to pass the time with some polite conversation, but I hate everything my parents stand for. If they weren't my parents, I'd be just as happy to see them fall off the edge of a very tall cliff. I really don't want to talk about them."

"Alright, alright. We'll talk about something else." He waved his hand in front of them, gesturing at the window. "Nice weather for flying today. Clear skies all the way. Nary a drop of rain."

After some silence, Ainsley asked, "What about your parents then?"

Eddie sucked in a long breath before he spoke. "They were protesting the first wave of expulsions. The demonstration turned violent. I was told it was hard to figure out what had happened after the fact because there were so many bodies, but they think a charging Qyntarak trampled my mother. When my dad tried to get to her, one of them knocked him down and he hit his head..."

His voice quavered as it trailed off.

Ainsley reached across and squeezed his shoulder. "They died heroes."

He turned his head away from her and wiped at his eyes.

After several minutes of silence, Eddie announced that they were coming to the scanning gate. The gate turned out to be four cables draped between the remains of crumbling apartment buildings. Eddie put the ship into a stable hover above the quadrilateral and opened an audio connection.

"We're all set down here," Wanda said. "Bring it down nice and slow, all the way below the wires. Then when I give you the word, just as slow going back up. That should give us a thorough scan that I can analyze."

"Roger that."

Eddie did as instructed, and they hovered above the makeshift scanner until Wanda's voice came back over Eddie's wrist computer.

"Everything looks good down here. But it's quite the piece of junk you picked out. How's it handle?"

"Like the beautiful workhorse that it is. Show a little respect."

"How's the power core holding up?"

"So far so good," Eddie said. "It has an upgraded Aldebaran solid fuel expansion core. Looks like the memory's been wiped, so I don't know how many cycles it's been through. The guy had it fully charged for us. I'm at 97% after flying here."

"That's not impressive given that you're flying with no load. I'll run some numbers. It should be good enough. I want us to have—"

"A few hours buffer. I know. We've discussed that to death already."

"No need to get snippy. You'll be the one flying that thing. I'll be safe and sound in the ops center. Just looking out for you."

Francis interjected, "You two done yammering? I don't like having this gate up any longer than necessary. Not to mention that an ancient cargo hauler hovering over it is conspicuous."

Eddie said, "Relax, big guy. There's nothing but squatters up here. As long as this isn't a Qyntarak ship, they don't care."

"Operational security best practices dictate that—"

"Okay. Got it. Moving on." Eddie tapped on his wrist computer to disconnect the call and turned to wink at Ainsley. "Time for the fun part."

"What's the fun part?"

CHAPTER 11

EDDIE PUSHED BOTH feet against the floor pedals and pulled back on the steering column. The cargo hauler took off in a steep climb that pressed Ainsley into her seat. Eddie screamed a yee-haw as they gained altitude. Ainsley wrapped her fingers around her chair's armrests and squeezed.

They kept climbing and even though the interior of the hauler had not gotten any louder, Eddie shouted when he asked her, "Having fun yet?"

"Not really."

He frowned. "I would've thought that with all the subterfuge and running around you do, you'd be more of a thrill seeker."

"I prefer my flights to involve a little more gravity control."

"There is zero excitement in that. Thrust flying is the greatest feeling in the world. Besides, you need a lot more money and much better connections than we have to get a black-market flyer with gravity control tech. I suppose you know more than most that the Qyntarak keep that technology heavily regulated." He paused as if in thought then added, "You don't—I mean, you wouldn't have that kind of connection, would you?"

"Oh, sure, every month we have Sunday dinner and talk about all the black-market gravity flyers that are available for purchase. Like any normal family."

Eddie grinned. "Just so you know, sarcasm is eventually going to get you into a misunderstanding with Francis. I just hope I'm there to see it. It'll be hilarious."

"I did notice he's not much for humor."

"Understatement of the year."

"What about Wanda? What's her deal?"

"Wanda? I think it's pretty self-evident that she is very much in favor of sarcasm."

"That's not what I meant and you know it."

"I know that's not what you mean. Not sure it's my place to tell her story. Give her a couple years to open up to you."

"A couple years seems optimistic."

"That's true," he said. "She was a kid. Her family was living in an evacuated town. The Qyntarak were clearing out the squatters. I assume you never experienced how they did things. They'd swoop into town, drive out any remaining people, and use their gravity weapons to level acres of land at a time so it could be reclaimed as green space. They make it sound positive on the newsfeeds but when it happens, it's not peaceful.

"I don't know how accurate her memory of the event is, after all, she was only a kid, but she says there were thousands of people resisting. In the chaos, she got trapped underneath one of the grav flyers. I don't pretend to understand even the fundamentals of how those gravity control flyers work, so I can't explain what happened except that somehow being that close to the gravity plate must've started rearranging things in her body. Her clothes started disintegrating and the pain was beyond description. She thinks that she tried to push it away from her, which is how she got those scars on her hands. She woke up from a coma weeks later, body mangled, her parents missing and assumed exiled. Now she's got a hatred for the Qyntarak burning in her so deep that she'll never be able to exact enough vengeance."

Eddie gave Ainsley a minute to let the story sink in. Finally, she said, "That's beyond awful. And then growing up without parents to help her cope with it. It must have been so hard."

"I imagine it was. Helped that she's a genius."

"Why hasn't she had reconstructive surgery? I mean, with nanobot injections and a couple medical bots, I would think they could make her look at least a little normal."

"I've been through a lot in my time. Taken a lot of risks. And even I'm not brave enough to broach that subject with her. Just between you and me though, my theory is that a piece of her wants the constant reminder so she doesn't lose her focus or forget why she hates the Qyntarak so much."

The depressing logic made sense to Ainsley, and she felt a bit of shame for her bitterness about her own childhood. She resented her parents but couldn't imagine trading places with Wanda. Her guilt soon morphed into anger and she had a newfound confidence in her decision to work with Miriam.

Eddie pointed to a display in front of them. "Power level's at 94% now. That's going down faster than I'd like. We need to go pick up some cargo and push this thing harder to be certain it'll hold up. Fortunately, I know a place."

He adjusted the controls and Ainsley felt the cargo hauler shift to the right, flying roughly northwest based on the position of the late afternoon sun.

Eddie opened an audio channel with the rest of the team and let them know what he was doing. The detour to test the power core would knock them off schedule and Eddie said he wouldn't want anyone to worry about them.

But Eddie forgot about the one other person who would be concerned about the amount of time they spent test driving the ship. An alarm sounded inside the cockpit and the voice of the slick-haired salesman came through the speakers.

"Mr. Fields, I'm just checking in since you've been gone for a while. Your test drive is running quite long. The location beacon in that vehicle shows that you are on your way north and getting pretty far outside the city. I do have some other interested buyers who are hoping to take that machine out for a drive before we close this afternoon."

Eddie had insisted on the fake name Edward Fields over Ainsley's protest that farmers with the last name Fields was too unbelievable. Eddie had winked at her and insisted that it was too outrageous for anyone to believe it was made up. Ainsley could tell from the tone of the salesman that he was doubting their cover.

"Yeah, we weren't planning to stay out this long but we couldn't help noticing that the power's draining kind of fast. And the memory's been wiped so I can't verify its duty cycle.

Since I need this for hauling lots of plants and soil, I'm just swinging up to a friend's place to confirm that the core holds up under load."

"I can assure you, Mr. Fields, we did rigorous testing on that power core. Standard part of our 191 point inspection process."

"Does that inspection process include wiping the memory of every core you sell?"

"Mr. Fields, I promise that is a top quality machine with a fully inspected power core. It will serve you for many long years. I tell you what, why don't you head on back and I'll do up the paperwork, and I'll even throw in an extra power core warranty to go along with it just for your peace of mind."

"I'm afraid I'm more of a look and see and test it out myself type of guy. We won't be long."

"I must insist that you come back right away, Mr. Fields. We don't authorize test drives beyond the city."

"Listen, my wife and I need something like this for our farming business. We're going to get up and running and then we're going to start a family. A family business means all hands are working. Do you want my darling little wife to be hovering 150 feet off the ground in a cargo hauler you sold us when a spent power core drops offline and she goes plummeting to the ground, orphaning my five children? Is that what you want? Instead of giving me an extra forty-five minutes to do a cargo test with one of the biggest purchases I'll make in my entire life?"

Eddie winked at Ainsley. She rolled her eyes at him.

"Of course not. But, Mr. Fields—"

"We'll be back in an hour. You go ahead and get that paperwork ready so we can close this deal after a quick cargo load test. Yes?"

There was a long pause and a heavy sigh from the cockpit speakers. "I will have the paperwork ready."

A brief melodic tone played to indicate that the salesman had disconnected the call.

"Darling little wife?"

"I was improvising. Just felt like something Edward Fields would say."

"Edward Fields is going to find himself farming alone if he keeps talking like that."

"Then I guess it's a good thing he won't exist after an anonymous currency token buys this puppy for us."

Eddie brought them down into a pit of rock and gravel.

"Where are we?"

"An old stone quarry. From back when the cities were still expanding and they needed rock for building material. We come out here to test explosives."

"And why are we here?"

"There are literally tons of massive boulders out here. We'll latch onto one to make sure we can fly up and maneuver with a giant rock hanging off us like a tail."

"I don't understand. How does that tell you if this thing can tow cars from a grav train?"

"When we decouple the cars from the grav train, there will be residual energy in the anti-gravity plates for a solid fifteen minutes. If we just unhooked them and let them go, they'd gradually drift to the ground. What we'll be doing is hooking to a segment of train cars and pulling them to where they can be unloaded before anyone can track us. Since the gravity plates will still be canceling out most of the train's mass, we won't really need that much power to pull them. Wanda did the math already. If we can pull one of these boulders around, we'll have more than enough power to haul the train cars."

He pointed through the windshield at a misshapen gray boulder split in half. "Francis and I did that. Split right down the middle with a shaped charge. Half of that will do nicely."

He swung the hauler around and landed within a few feet of the boulder.

They disembarked and Ainsley helped wrap cables and anchors around the half sphere until Eddie declared it well secured.

"Best not to trust the autopilot to take off for this one." Eddie increased power to the thrusters. "We don't want to learn the hard way that it doesn't have adaptive sensors and end up ripping the ship in half."

Eddie's tone was light but his words made Ainsley uneasy.

They rose from the quarry and Eddie commented several times on how well the hauler was handling the load. "This old boat is surprisingly responsive. I bet we can even take it through some maneuvers."

Before Ainsley could ask what he meant by maneuvers, Eddie accelerated into a tight turn and started gaining elevation. Behind them, she heard creaking and felt the ship shudder as it strained to bring itself and a chunk of the planet higher into the atmosphere.

"Oh, yeah," Eddie shouted. "Yee haw! That's how you get it done."

The acceleration forced Ainsley against her seat again. She couldn't help but grin, swept up in the thrill of Eddie's contagious excitement. He twisted the steering column and they banked to the left. She was about to give her own whoop of exhilaration when something made a loud pop and the ship lurched. It tipped from a left turn to a lean to the right as the lights went out in the cockpit and Ainsley lifted from her seat. Only the restraints kept her from drifting to the ceiling.

"What's happening?" she screamed.

Eddie hammered buttons and flipped switches but nothing was responding. He seemed to be acting out of desperation. "We lost the power core. 191 point inspection my ass."

He unbuckled his restraints and grabbed a handhold above him. "Come on. We need to bail out."

She yelled as she followed his lead. "Bail out? While we're spinning and falling? We won't be able to jump clear."

"The alternative is staying here and getting killed for sure. Evac packs are right behind us."

He pulled the first pack from the wall and gave it to Ainsley. She slid her arms through the openings and hit the activate button. Eddie pulled the strap for the second evac pack and the compartment came away empty.

Eddie's eyes went wide.

"Where's the other pack?" Ainsley shouted.

Without answering, Eddie hit the flashing red button next to Ainsley and squeezed a handhold with his other hand. A buzzer sounded and the door opened. Before Ainsley could say anything else, Eddie had his foot on her midsection and the air was forced out of her lungs as he shoved her into the howling wind.

She couldn't focus on anything as she tumbled out of control. It took her several gasping attempts to get a breath of air into her lungs. She felt the vest automatically constrict around her and it beeped and hissed as sensors and micro propellant jets stabilized her fall enough for the pack to release its parachute. Things whirred and clicked as the emergency evacuation pack brought her descent under control.

The boulder came loose and the cargo hauler wobbled as it fell back toward the mouth of the quarry pit. She saw no sign of Eddie.

A gust spun Ainsley and she lost sight of the falling ship.

She didn't hear the sound of its crash over the wind rushing past her ears. She looked down and saw that she was heading toward a large pond. There was a way to steer these packs. She'd heard the instructions dozens of times during the safety presentations on flights, but she'd never paid much attention to those. Things didn't crash. The safety briefings were just outdated paranoia, or so she had thought.

Point your toes, that's what they said. *Point your toes to where you want to land and the pack will do the rest.*

Pointing her toes caused her body weight to shift and the evac pack reacted. She landed in the muck at the edge of the pond, and the parachute fell into the water behind her. The vest released the cables attached to the chute and loosened its constricting hold.

She vomited into the mud and weeds at her feet. Her instinct was to curl up in a ball and cry, but she knew that would do no good. She touched her new wrist computer, the one Eddie had promised was more durable and secure than her old personal bracelet computer. She opened a team-wide channel.

"Hello? Help! Someone, please. We've had an accident."

Wanda answered first. "Ainsley, what happened? Are you

alright?"

"The hauler died on us. There was only one parachute. Eddie... Eddie tossed me out with it on. He went down with..."

She couldn't bring herself to say it.

Eddie had gone down.

The urge to vomit came back. She started to heave but forced herself to keep talking.

"It's a miracle that I'm—I can't believe he—"

"What? You can't believe that I pushed you out of a crashing plane? Give me a couple minutes to get the straps and things cleaned up over here and I'll come pick you up."

"Eddie?" Wanda said. "What's going on? We're all kinds of busy right now. I don't have time for your shenanigans."

Ainsley wanted to ask something. *How? How was Eddie alive?* She saw the ship tumbling into the quarry. But she couldn't form words. She was sobbing and felt like she was about to collapse.

"No shenanigans. Ainsley's right, we sort of crashed. The power core on this thing is a piece of crap. My guess is that if we cracked it open, what's on the inside doesn't match the label on the outside. Guess I know why the salesman didn't want me to bring it out here for a load test. Slimy son of a bitch. Pretty near killed me."

"Should I go kick the shit out of him?" Francis asked.

"Nah, I don't see what good that would do. If I held a grudge against everybody who almost killed me, there'd be no one left for me to talk to."

"What do you want to do then?" Wanda asked.

"I'm sort of partial to this boat now. Once the core came back online, it handled itself like a champ. I was able to reposition and make an emergency stop before it hit the ground. And that's with a governor module on the AI. I got a feeling we should just keep this one. Put in a new power core, of course. After crashing and almost killing me, I'm sure the price will be mighty fine. Wanda, you think you could come out here to disable the tracker and the kill switch?"

"Yeah, sure. Might as well get it over with."

"Great. Thanks. We'll wait here and call the asshole who nearly killed me. Ainsley, I'll come get you first. You're alright otherwise, yes?"

Ainsley had gotten her sobbing under control while the others talked. She could tell that she was in shock and was having trouble getting her body to do what her brain wanted it to.

"Ainsley? Ainsley, you still there?"

All she managed was, "How the hell are you still alive?"

CHAPTER 12

AINSLEY SPENT THE evening sitting in front of the fireplace and working her way through a bottle of corn whiskey. It really wasn't cold enough to justify having a fire burning, but Miriam had insisted that it would be therapeutic. Ainsley's hands had stopped shaking hours earlier and fatigue was setting in.

Eddie, Miriam, and Francis were busy with the cargo hauler, which Eddie had ultimately procured for one-tenth the asking price and a promise not to report the illegal modifications that nearly killed Edward Fields and his darling little wife. Undocumented sales on the black market were one thing. Endangerment of life caused by modifying and misrepresenting a piece of heavy equipment was a different matter. The salesman knew that he risked going to a red ship if Eddie pressed the issue. Not that Eddie would ever be able to report him, but the salesman didn't know that.

Even though Eddie had explained how he'd regained control of the cargo hauler when it was meters away from slamming into the rocky bottom of the quarry pit, Ainsley struggled to wrap her head around it. In the seconds she'd been tumbling through the air, he'd brought the power core back online, rebooted the system, and strapped in before the computer performed an automatic emergency landing. His composure during and after the incident made her wonder if his ability to function under such extreme stress was innate or learned. Whichever it was, it was a reminder for her not to underestimate the members of her new team.

Her mind was swimming from the alcohol when Eddie sat beside her and began rearranging smoldering logs with a poker.

"Listen," he said, "I'm sorry about earlier."

"Sorry? You didn't screw with the energy core. You saved my life. I would've just stood there trying to figure out what to do without an evac pack. If you hadn't pushed me out…"

"I shouldn't have even gone up without knowing that there were two packs charged and in working condition. And I never should've flown the ship like that so quickly. And I shouldn't have done it with you on board at all. It was reckless. I was treating it too much like a game. And it nearly got both of us killed. So I'm sorry."

"It's not necessary, but thank you. It doesn't change the fact that you saved my life."

He lifted the open whiskey bottle from the floor and took a long pull, his nose wrinkling from the sting of first contact with the alcohol.

"Man, Miriam really gave you the cheap stuff. Shit."

"Booze is booze."

"Cheers to that."

"I was wondering," Ainsley said. "Do you think it's too late to have Francis go down and kick that guy's ass?"

Eddie started to laugh and then grimaced. "Aw, crap, it went up my nose. Piss and hell, that burns."

Ainsley couldn't help but laugh while he wiped his watering eyes.

When he'd composed himself, Eddie said, "Normally, I think Francis would be thrilled to head over there and beat that guy senseless for you. Now that we've got the ship, though, we have a lot of work to do. Clock's ticking."

"Meanwhile, I feel useless until I'm back at the warehouse."

"Well, good news. The other reason I came to check on you was to make sure you don't drink yourself into a coma. You do not want to be hungover tomorrow. Wanda's setting up simulations for you so she can teach you how to install her AI virus thing into the computer systems at the warehouse. After getting a glimpse of what she has in store for you, I can guarantee you will not want to have a headache."

EDDIE WAS RIGHT—Ainsley did not want to have a headache, but she did. And Wanda didn't try to hide her irritation with Ainsley's sluggishness. Nevertheless, they persevered together for hours until Wanda was convinced that Ainsley was prepared.

During that night's shift, her only job was to identify the computer terminals she would need to access and to mentally walk through the many steps. She also needed to pay attention to who was paying attention to her.

Ben Triggs supervised two dozen workers divided into three teams of eight. Each team had a lead who doled out the work that had been given to them by Triggs. (She'd taken to thinking of him as Triggs instead of Ben because it softened the guilt she was feeling about betraying his trust.)

Ainsley was on Kamil's team. He had a good rapport with Triggs and she hoped that would work to her advantage. If Triggs had confidence in Kamil, he wouldn't concern himself with what Ainsley was doing, even if she was at a computer terminal where she didn't belong. Kamil was a competent coordinator for his small team, and he wasn't a micromanager. That was also going to work to Ainsley's advantage.

The one thing not working in her favor was the prowling stare of her coworker Valentin. She could sense his eyes following her whenever she was in his field of vision. Her instincts told her he was a creep. Keeping him at a distance was often on her mind. It was an annoying complication to have someone watching her movements. She had half a mind to ask Francis to stage a mugging and leave him out of commission for a few weeks, but she felt guilty just for having the thought.

In the last few minutes of her shift, Ainsley stopped at a tablet mounted on an articulating arm and went through her mental checklist. This was where she would perform the most time-consuming tasks—entering commands to connect the virus to a litany of subsystems. The position was well obstructed by shipping containers, and it was far away from both Kamil's preferred workstation and Triggs's makeshift office constructed from stacked containers.

"Ainsley?"

The voice made her jump and she was partway through whirling around before she remembered to keep her expression neutral and innocent-looking.

"Mr. Triggs. I mean, Ben. You startled me."

"Didn't mean to. People usually hear me coming. Heavy footsteps and all that."

She faked a casual smile. "Right."

"I know shift is almost up but I noticed you seem to be lounging around back here. I'm a relaxed guy when I can be but I insist on my team being productive for their entire shift."

Her lie came effortlessly, assembled from a scaffolding of truths. "I'm sorry. I had a bit of a traumatic experience on my days off. A friend was driving manually and nearly killed us. I'm still a bit shaken from it. And exhausted because of that."

The giant of a man considered her. When he didn't break eye contact and tilted his head to match the angle of hers, Ainsley knew he was buying her story.

"How's your friend?"

"Totally fine. Amazingly."

"And the car?"

"Pretty banged up. But salvageable, I think. Something internal needs to be replaced. I don't know much about cars so not sure how serious it is."

Ainsley reminded herself not to ramble. She didn't want to overdo it.

"What kind of car? Manual steering is getting rare outside of illegal cabs."

Her brain went into overdrive trying to remember the

type of car they'd taken to the sales lot and if it had manual controls. She couldn't recall. Ainsley knew nothing about cars but the persona she'd built was a chronically curious person—the type of person who would ask something about a car, especially the novelty of a manually driven one.

"I have no idea. I'm really not into cars."

He looked into the distance for a fraction of a second then back at her. "Well, I hope it's not too expensive to fix. Back to work, alright?"

"Yes, sir."

"Ben. You think I don't like Mr. Triggs, imagine how I feel about sir."

She turned in the direction of Valentin and a few others who were moving food ration bars from a large container into a crate for an automated pod launch. Triggs's glance at the end bothered her. He didn't buy her story. Not entirely. How could she have been so stupid to not keep track of where Triggs was? It was sloppy.

She looked to where he'd glanced. Kamil stood hunched over his workstation.

CHAPTER 13

"Kamil, come by my office before you leave after shift, will you?"

"You got it, boss."

Ben's chair groaned when he let his bulk drop into it. He pulled up the access records for the warehouse computer systems, starting with the terminal where Ainsley had been loitering. Maybe she'd been sending personal messages on work time and didn't want to get caught.

The search showed nothing. She had not accessed a terminal for hours. The team was loading for a launch so that at least made sense. What didn't make sense to him was her hiding back there. If she needed a moment, she could have taken a bathroom break. Or was he reading too much into it? Putting too much stock in his ability to read a person? Her story didn't sound insincere, just implausible. Maybe he stressed her out. It wouldn't be the first time his size made someone uncomfortable.

From up in the high rafters, unseen speakers played a melody to announce the end of shift. Soon after, a cacophony of voices called out farewells and wishes for a good night, even though it was now early morning and the sun outside would already be driving away the chill of the night air. That was Ben's favorite part of working the night shift. Instead of exiting in the dreary dusk, he got to walk out into sunlight.

When the parade of departing footsteps had ended, Kamil knocked on the side of a container that served as a wall for Ben's tiny workspace.

"You wanted to see me?"

"Yes, about Ainsley. How's she doing?"

"So far so good. No complaints from me. Below average speed loading and unloading but holds her own, and I'm sure she'll improve with practice. Polite, follows instructions well, no trouble picking up the computer work."

"Any issues with getting tasks completed? Signs of distraction or stress?"

"Not that I've noticed. Why? Is the data telling you something I'm missing?"

"No, nothing like that. I found her loitering in a corner. Gave her a little speech about expecting everyone to work their whole shift. She told me a story about being in a car accident and being rattled from it. I don't know. Something about it isn't sitting right with me."

"You mean like a car having an accident? What are the odds of that?"

"She said it was manual drive, something her friend had."

"Manual drive? That's a death wish. She's not right in the head if she's running in that kind of crowd."

"You remember how we used to joke about moles coming in from central office?"

Kamil chuckled. "Spies come to ferret out the petty thieves skimming from the shipments and threatening the great wheels of economic progress."

Ben pressed his palms to the top of his desk and used his arms to help push his big frame to a standing position. "I'm sure I'm just being paranoid, but I didn't like the way she was hanging around a secluded terminal and throwing out a wacky story. We have that big shipment of retrofit supplies coming soon. Some of that's sensitive material. It's not completely insane to imagine central office checking in on things to make sure we're ready to deal with it."

"You checked her computer logs?"

"Yeah, nothing."

"Well, with all the bureaucracy and double-talk you wade through trying to find your wife, I'm guessing your imagination is just getting the better of you."

Ben gave a loud sigh. "You're probably right. Do me a favor, though, and pay close attention. Let me know if you notice anything off."

THE SUN OUTSIDE the warehouse was stronger than normal, prompting Ben to take a moment to turn his face toward it, eyes closed, and to feel its warmth on his face. He didn't need to rush. His meeting with Restitution Affairs wasn't for another fifty minutes, and he wouldn't feel like enjoying anything after that.

Gwen was up there. He felt it. He just wanted someone to confirm it, to give him a modicum of hope, and to let him move on from finding her to finding a way to be with her again.

The ache was as potent as it had ever been. He missed her so much.

THE REPRESENTATIVE OF Restitution Affairs was as opposite to Ben as he could imagine someone being. She was at least two feet shorter than his six feet eight inches. Her blonde hair framed a gaunt face, and she gave him a cheerful greeting before listening to him with rapt attention.

Ben told his story and she nodded along. She swiped on a screen, logging his inquiry and starting a search for information. He'd only been there for a minute when she made a final nod and looked him in the eye.

"I am afraid that you are not entitled to any compensation."

"I'm not looking for compensation. Just information. No one will tell me what happened to Gwen."

She looked to the computer display and then at Ben again. He wasn't making any effort to hide his despair, and the look on his face must have made her uncomfortable because she looked away again and pulled at the sleeve of her cheap cotton shirt.

The clerk found her resolve and looked back up at him. "Sir, this is the Restitution Affairs office. It is not an information bureau. We aren't a lost and found. I can't help you." Then she added, "I'm sorry."

Ben put his large hands against the glass barrier and leaned in close to the circle through which they spoke to each other. "Please, can you just look? I only want to know where she is. That's all."

Despite the partition between them, the clerk looked

nervous. Ben was aware that he intimidated people even when he didn't mean to be threatening. And he saw in her expression that it had lost him any chance of further empathy.

"I'm sorry too," he whispered.

He slammed the base of his fist against the window and it rattled ominously. He turned and hurried away before security personnel showed up to escort him out.

He found a rusted bench and collapsed onto it. Grasping his head between his hands, he rocked back and forth, squeezing his eyes shut and willing the desperation not to leak out.

CHAPTER 14

No one tried to hide their disappointment with Ainsley. Miriam told her to lie low for several days and stressed that they needed her system access to be valid when the train was arriving. It was paramount that she not arouse any suspicion that might cause her to lose her computer privileges.

She slept most of the day and was eating alone in preparation for another trip to the warehouse when Eddie eased into the seat across the table from her.

"I want to tell you a story. I think it might help." He took a heavy drink of the amber liquid in his glass. "I was doing a job when I was younger. A legit paying job, doing neighborhood cleanup."

Ainsley looked up with surprise. "An expulsion?"

"Cleanup. They deployed a bunch of humans after an expulsion to make sure there were no squatters in the buildings before the Qyntarak came in to level the place.

Hey, don't look at me like that. Everyone's got to eat.

"Anyway, I was clearing an apartment and there was this yellow toy on the floor. And taped to the wall was a picture, something a little kid would draw. It was a stick person holding the same yellow toy in its hand, and then off to the side there was this smudgy part that I think was supposed to be a Qyntarak, and on the ground around it were more stick men with their eyes crossed out. I stood there staring, wondering what kind of shit this kid had seen that they would draw that.

"So I'm frozen there, and remember that this whole area was cleared already, we were only doing a final sweep, but while I'm standing there looking at that photo, there's movement behind me and before I can turn around, someone cracks me on the back of the head and the room goes fuzzy. I have a vague memory of someone running away, or at least I think I remember that, maybe it's an invented memory, I don't know. I totally lost my bearings for a while and when I didn't respond to calls from my team over the comm, the company sent in a search party for me. They found me, dragged me out, treated my head injury, made sure I was all patched up, and then they fired me. And to add insult to literal injury, they charged me for the search and rescue plus the rehabilitation services.

"I was just a kid doing grunt work, and the bill was astronomical. It would've taken me a decade to repay it. That kind of debt is a slippery slope. I mean, if I'd had a second accident while I was trying to pay off that debt, that's it, I'd end up in forced labor on a red ship. The modern day debt slave. All because I wasn't paying attention to what was happening around me. A couple seconds nearly ruined the rest of my life."

Ainsley realized she'd been holding her spoon in midair the entire time that Eddie talked. She returned it to her bowl. "So what did you do?"

"About two years later, I took my first payment to look the other way while something went missing on a job site. That eventually led me to Miriam and now I'm more than debt free."

Ainsley wanted to ask Eddie where the line was. And which lines he'd crossed before, or if he would again, but she was too afraid to ask. If Eddie thought she was losing her nerve, he'd have to go to Miriam. Ainsley didn't know what would happen if he did.

She slid her chair back and stood from the table. "I have to get going for my shift. Thank you for sharing that with me."

He swirled his whiskey, which he'd been fiddling with but hadn't touched while telling his story. "I hope it helps. Keep your wits. Stay sharp. Pay attention to everything that's happening around you. Everything. And it'll be fine."

He emptied his glass with a single gulp and waved her off.

WITHOUT THE STRESS of finding opportunities to slip away for covert activity, work in the warehouse was monotonous, a welcome break from the escalating busyness of the days and evenings while the crew pushed to complete final preparations for the job.

By the end of her six-day rotation, Ainsley had a grasp on the routines and weaknesses of the warehouse teams.

She spent three days helping pack supplies onto the cargo hauler, which Eddie and Miriam double and triple checked.

There were seven hours left before Ainsley had to be back at the warehouse when Miriam clapped her hands several times and called for everyone to gather.

"We're ready. The plan is a go. Good work, everyone. Ainsley, you need to get some rest. You have to work all night and then tomorrow will be a long day. Here." She pressed a pill into the palm of Ainsley's hand. "This is an REM booster. It'll make sure you get to sleep and that it's good quality rest. I don't know about you, but I tend to be a bit jittery trying to sleep before a job."

Ainsley held the pill between her thumb and index finger and raised it in the air like she was making a toast with a miniature glass. "See you all in the sky tomorrow."

The effects of the pill came on quickly, and Ainsley's vision had gone wavy before she'd even made it to her bed. She collapsed on the luxurious mattress and let the medication drag her off to sleep. She dreamed of yellow toy trains circling her like a swarm of insects. One hovered in front of her face and it sprouted six long tentacles that reached for her. She struggled to lean away but she was paralyzed. The tentacles forced their way into her ears, nostrils, and mouth. She tried to scream but they'd wrapped around her tongue. All she could manage was a weak moan.

The alarm from her wrist computer was a relief. She sat up, feeling rested, but her hands were shaking.

CHAPTER 15

DESPITE HER RACING mind, nothing was out of place as Ainsley made her way to the staging warehouse. The queue at the security checkpoint was quiet as usual. She felt an irrational fear that the security guards could see inside her head and knew what she was going to do that night, but they looked as bored as ever when she passed.

Triggs and Kamil were twenty feet ahead of her. She slowed, letting the distance grow so she wouldn't have to engage with them. She was ready with small talk—an entire narrative of her days off—but she'd save that for when she needed it. There was no reason for her to go looking for conversation. Her chatty, inquisitive persona would require her to be a lot more talkative than she wanted right now.

When they had about two hours remaining in their shift, Triggs called everyone in for a team meeting. The two dozen workers huddled in a mass around their boss. Valentin positioned himself so he was standing too close to her. She balled her hand into a fist. If she wasn't on mission, if today wasn't the day, she just might...

Triggs was explaining that a large shipment was coming in. "We have to push all the standard stock back, stacked high against the west wall. This is a high priority, off-schedule delivery that dayshift is loading and launching today. We need to make sure they have lots of room to work. So take a short break, get a coffee and take a piss, and then get in an exoskeleton suit and start moving crates."

While the others left for their break, Ainsley waited for an opening. When Triggs waved Kamil and the other team leads into his office, she saw her chance. She rushed to the computer terminal in the back corner and pried off the heel of her left boot. In the hollow shoe bottom was a data vault, smaller than a fingernail, which she peeled away.

She authenticated her identity, entered a sequence of commands from Wanda, and pressed the tiny data storage device against the terminal's sensor. A progress bar appeared on the display as the data transferred from the vault to the computer system.

1%.

3%.

While she waited, Ainsley stomped her boot on the floor to reset the heel.

7%.

The data vault was small but held an incredible amount of data. It took time to move that much data from one physical device to another. Then the AI would have to initialize itself and spread into the network. Wanda had tried to explain to Ainsley why it would take so long but in the end she'd shrugged and said, "Don't worry about it, it's physics."

Ainsley wanted to look around, to ensure that no one was watching her, but that would make her appear more suspicious.

53%.

"Come on," she whispered.

She heard voices from across the warehouse. Either the first of the workers were returning from their break or the team leads had finished their meeting with Triggs.

64%.

More voices. The others were definitely coming back from break. The time on the terminal told her this was taking longer than Wanda had predicted.

Not good.

71%.

Her free hand started to twitch against her leg and she had to concentrate to make it stop. The voices grew louder.

77%.

There was a T-intersection in the walkways between the stacks of crates. The teams would have to turn right to get to the exoskeleton suits. She was to the left. The voices should get louder and then fade when the group turned away from her.

86%.

The voices and footsteps started to grow quieter.

91%.

Then a single set of footsteps. They got louder, coming closer, and Ainsley hovered one finger over the cancel button on the screen while the thumb of her other hand held the data vault in place.

97%.

The footsteps stopped.

Ainsley held her breath.

99%.

100%.

Operation complete.

A messaging app opened automatically. That was good. The warehouse computer systems had personal messaging apps disabled but Wanda's virus included its own that could tunnel through the computer network's security filters.

She typed in the message: EGGS FOR BREAKFAST?

The reply was almost instantaneous: REQUIRES WORKING GRIDDLE. HOLD ON.

The coded response meant the virus had propagated itself and Wanda was able to communicate with it. Wanda would be finishing a series of diagnostic checks and would signal Ainsley when it was safe for her to destroy the data vault and log out of the computer.

"What is this now?"

Ainsley's eyes rolled up and her spirit sagged in unison.

"Go away, Valentin."

"You have not worked here long but you know the rules, no? Computers are not for personal use. And messaging apps aren't allowed."

"I'm just making plans with my boyfriend for breakfast." She emphasized the word boyfriend, hoping that would be enough to deter the cretin.

Once again, he moved in until he was uncomfortably close. "I'm sure, I'm sure. Nevertheless, the rules are the rules. It would be a shame to lose a job so quickly. I mean, after all, it might be that you simply didn't realize that the rules applied to break time."

"How about you forget that you saw me here and I'll owe you one."

She still had her back to him and wished she could see his face, but she wouldn't risk taking her eyes off the terminal. Not yet.

"I don't care for credit. Don't like people owing me things. I prefer to take payment upfront, I'm sure you understand."

He pressed in closer and it made her skin crawl. She knew at least three ways that she could leave him incapacitated and in pain, but she couldn't take that chance when she was so close to completing her mission. Instead, she spun in place, fighting against her instincts in order to appear compliant. She placed one hand against his chest and applied enough pressure to halt his advance.

"Not here, silly. After shift. Wait for me by security."

She slid the data vault into a pocket with her left hand while she ran her right hand up from his chest to his cheek where she stroked it several times with her thumb. She could see in his eyes that she was feeding his power lust. She felt sick to her stomach for it, but he backed off and waved a finger.

"End of shift, we'll have some fun."

As soon as he was out of sight, she spun back to the terminal where a new message waited: GRIDDLE IS WORKING.

She exhaled a deep breath. Less than two hours to go. She could do this.

A couple hours in the exoskeleton suits kept Valentin from getting too close or handsy with her. Although Ainsley would have taken an opportunity to knee him in the groin, the mission was her priority and she was thankful that he couldn't force her into a situation in which she'd have to choose. It would be harder for her to sneak out after taking down Valentin.

Ten minutes before quitting time, the call came from Triggs for everyone to return their exoskeleton suits to the charging bays. He said that even though they hadn't quite finished, it was close enough. Dayshift could finish up before the shipment arrived. A tingle of excitement ran down Ainsley's spine. The shipment would never arrive.

As the others made their way back in ones and twos, Ainsley kept working. She had to give them time to get out of their suits and clear the area so she could return her depleted suit and switch into a fully charged one.

A direct call from Triggs came through the exo suit's communicator. "Ainsley, is that you still out there?"

"Yeah, it's me. Just moving a few more crates. I don't like leaving a job almost finished."

"I can respect that. Just remember that you don't make overtime. Doesn't matter when you actually clock out, your pay stops at the top of the hour."

"I know. But you've got to be extra if you want to make supervisor some day, right?"

Triggs laughed. "Hard work will get you to supervisor and no farther. You have to be lazy to go any higher than that."

Now they were both laughing. "Just six more crates here and my section will be clear. Then I'll call it a day."

"Copy that."

The last few workers were walking away from the charging station as Ainsley approached. They waved to her and one lady giggled when Ainsley responded with a cartoonish wave using the oversized hands of the exo suit.

Getting out of a suit was easier with two people but they were designed for solo use. Using a quick release mechanism, the operator could get an arm free and loosen the safety restraints around the arms, torso, and legs before pulling a release on the harness that held the wearer in place. Ainsley was working on the top leg strap when someone else's hand unexpectedly ran up her thigh.

"Here, let me help you with that."

Ainsley jerked to move away from Valentin and the exoskeleton followed her lead, the free arm swinging out of control as she stumbled back.

"Whoa, whoa, whoa! Be careful. I was just trying to help."

Her voice was almost a hiss when she replied. "I said by the security checkpoint."

"I was concerned we might miss each other in the crowd."

He tried to move closer to her again and she backhanded him with the arm of the suit that was still attached. It pushed him against the frame of the charging station with a thump.

"Oh, you like it a little rough do you?"

Ainsley didn't hesitate. The suit's hands were humanlike but couldn't form a proper fist. Nevertheless, she squeezed its digits as best she could and drove it into Valentin's face. She heard a crunch and a pop followed by the crack of his head hitting a post. His body slumped to the floor. She hurried to release herself from the rest of the restraints and dropped to the ground. She pressed two fingers against his wrist and then his neck until she found a pulse.

He was still alive.

The limited feedback of the exoskeleton suit made it hard for her to judge how hard she had hit him, but she assumed he'd be out for a while and concussed when he did come around. That should be plenty of time for her to get out of the warehouse.

She strapped into a new suit and starting jogging.

Taking advantage of the exoskeleton's amplification of her movements, Ainsley jumped container to container, climbing crates she'd arranged like an oversized set of stairs. With a utility blade built into the suit, she cut away the seals around a window and pried the plates of double-pane glass free, leaning everything against the wall slowly so it wouldn't break.

The early morning air was cool and damp, and Ainsley shivered involuntarily as she steered the suit through the opening. The maintenance walkway outside the window was only a few feet wide and the handrail wasn't designed for the extra height of an exo suit. Ainsley tried to ignore the possibility of a gust of wind pushing her over the railing.

She moved as quickly as she dared to a landing and jumped across the eight foot gap to the flat roof of an adjacent building.

Eddie had dropped a camouflaged case on the roof the day before with a drone. She scooped it up with one hand of the exo suit and released her other arm so she could use her fingers to open it. Nestled in foam inside was a communicator that she stuck in her ear.

"I'm in place."

"Roger that. ETA twenty-five seconds."

Ainsley tossed the camouflaged case aside and turned to face eastward. The glow of the rising sun was on the horizon, and it caused a hopeful feeling to well up in her chest.

This is working, she thought. They were going to do it.

She heard the rumbling thrust of the cargo hauler a few

seconds later. It slowed to a drifting hover and dropped a cable to her. Ainsley grabbed the tether and guided the disk at its end to the bulky section of the suit around her waist. It was clumsy work in the exoskeleton but the electromagnetic lock snapped on with contact. When the cable pulled taut, it dragged Ainsley into the air with enough force that it made her grunt with discomfort.

CHAPTER 16

KAMIL SET HIS cup on the corner of Ben's desk. "You think the coffee we send up is better quality than what they give us in here?"

"I hope so," Ben said. "If not, one of these days someone up there will get fed up and drop a rock on our heads."

Ben swallowed the dregs from the bottom of his own cup and wrinkled his nose at the gritty texture. "Alright, let's get out of here. Has Ainsley clocked out?"

Kamil swiped his wrist computer and shook his head side to side. "No. That's odd."

"I don't care what she's trying to prove, she needs to pack up and go home. Dayshift's gonna need the floor."

"The logs show that she returned the exo suit she was using and checked out a fresh one about fifteen minutes ago."

"What the hell has gotten into her? Where is she now?"

Kamil studied the display on his wrist and frowned. "Odd. The second suit she checked out is showing as out of range."

"Out of range? That's impossible. Let me check the surveillance footage."

Ben tapped at the screen on his desk and received a warning message that he was already logged in elsewhere.

"That's not right," he said. "My last session should've timed out in the time we've been talking. Can you see where I'm logged in?"

"Just a second." Kamil tapped and swiped for several seconds. "You seem to be logged in everywhere and nowhere."

"I don't understand."

"Something weird is going on with your account. We need to—hold on, your account just registered dozens of no-fly zones due to environmental emergency conditions."

Kamil touched his wrist computer against the display on Ben's desk and a map filled the screen.

"That's us here. This is the route for the train bringing the delivery. These orange areas, your account logged as no-fly."

"They're rerouting the train."

Kamil traced his finger along the display. "I think you're right. Like a channel through cliffs. Only one way for the water to flow."

"The train's autopilot will drop into low-speed mode when it's forced off course. Shit. Somebody's hitting the train."

"That's insane," Kamil said. "Nobody's dumb enough to go after a Qyntarak shipment. It's suicide."

"Well, someone's doing it. Call this into security. I'm going after them."

CHAPTER 17

"I LIKE THIS thing." Francis squeezed his left hand and watched the mechanical hand of the exoskeleton mimic his movement. "This will make my part of the job a snap."

Ainsley's stomach lurched sideways as the cargo hauler decelerated without warning.

"We're in place," Eddie said. "Clock's ticking."

Ainsley reconnected the tether cable to the exoskeleton suit that Francis was now wearing. He jumped and landed on the roof of the grav train below. Watching him fall, she flashed back to when Eddie had pushed her out the door with the evac pack. She glanced at the wall where both packs were missing. If they crashed today…

"Hold on tight." The ship surged ahead as Eddie sent power to the thrusters. "Dropping the clamping cable."

Through the open door, Ainsley and Miriam watched one end of a heavy cable drop like a stone on a string until it met the top of a train car.

Eddie shouted over the roar of the wind and thrusters, which was unnecessary because they all wore communicators, and his voice was painfully loud in Ainsley's ear. "Firing secondary cable."

A thinner cable shot from a launcher that Eddie had mounted next to the door. The magnet on the free end of the cable made contact with the train and the launcher retracted the excess slack back into itself until the cable was tight.

"We have good contact on clamping and secondary cables," Eddie said, his voice still too loud over the comm.

Miriam hefted the box in her hands and pushed it against the secondary cable until it locked in place. She unclipped her tether cable from the frame of the cargo ship, moved it to the hook on the box, and jumped. The mechanism controlled her descent so that her landing on the train roof was almost elegant. They'd practiced this maneuver dozens of times, but Ainsley wasn't looking forward to it. She repeated Miriam's actions and reminded herself not to scream as she dropped.

The train had twenty-three cars. They were taking seventeen of them. The first five were fuel cells and low value goods being transferred between warehouses. The last car was a stabilizing unit that prevented the train from drifting too far out of level. Ainsley's job was to take out the coupling between the fifth and sixth cars. Then Francis would break the connection with the stabilizing unit at the back, allowing Eddie to pull the free-floating cars away. Once disconnected, they'd have fifteen minutes of residual anti-gravity. Eddie would need to haul ass as soon as Francis finished.

Miriam and Ainsley moved to the gap between cars five and six. Miriam said, "Wanda, I'm in position."

"Good. Touch your wrist computer against the door sensor in three, two, one."

Miriam tapped her arm to a black square and the door slid open, revealing the interior of the train compartment.

She looked at Ainsley. "Give me two minutes. When I confirm the contents, take out that coupling."

The door shut behind Miriam, and Ainsley set to work.

Her pack held three industrial pop boxes. They would compromise the coupling without putting a hole in the train itself. She tried not to think about how much destructive potential was strapped to her back.

Not wanting to drop an explosive, and really not wanting to fall, she moved with care. They were hundreds of feet off the ground. Under the circumstances, there was no way Eddie would be able to save her if she fell this time.

The final pop box was almost in place when Miriam's voice announced that she had confirmed the cargo. "Blow the coupling."

Ainsley finished and tightened the straps of her pack. She grasped a handhold to climb out of the blast zone when something powerful wrapped around her throat. She kicked and swung her arms with no effect. She imagined a Qyntarak, one of its unearthly tentacles tightening around her neck and squeezing. Instead, she heard a man's voice.

"What are you doing?"

Triggs?

Over the communicator, Eddie shouted, "Shit, Ainsley's got company. Where did he come from?"

"On my way," Francis said.

Miriam answered, "Francis, you need to be ready to disconnect the stabilizer."

"It won't matter if she can't blow that coupling." Francis was breathing hard. He must already be running across the tops of the trains.

"Let me go," Ainsley said.

"I can't. Not when you're going to hurt people."

"We're not hurting people. We're getting back at those monsters. They've taken everything. We're taking it back."

"I thought you understood how things work. The stuff we send up into orbit helps humans."

"Upgrading Qyntarak ships isn't helping any humans."

With his free arm, Triggs banged his wrist computer on the same black panel Miriam had used and the door opened again. Triggs dragged Ainsley into the train with one arm, but loosened his grip when he realized that he was choking her.

"Read the labels."

She looked at a crate in front of her: BEDDING - HUMAN SINGLE.

The next stack read: RECYCLER FILTERS - EARTH ATMO.

Another said: NO-STATIC ORTHO CUSHIONED - MENS SIZES 8-10.

Ainsley looked at Triggs with confusion.

"If you keep going, you'll find antiviral medication and components for repairs for one of the old exile ships."

"I don't understand," she said. "They told me—this isn't what we were supposed to be taking."

"These supplies are for a human exile ship. My wife is up there on one of them. It could be her ship. I won't let you take them."

"There must be a mistake. Let me talk to the others." She

tapped the communicator in her ear to open a channel to the entire team. "Everyone, I'm inside the train. These aren't Qyntarak supplies. They're for an exile ship. Bedding, air filters, shoes, medicine. We have to call this off."

It was Miriam who replied. "We don't have time to discuss this right now. The job is the job. Ainsley, blow that coupling."

Ainsley stared at her hands. It surprised her to see that they weren't shaking. "I won't."

Miriam made a growling sound and Eddie said, "Francis, you need take care of this. Hurry."

"Copy that."

Ainsley muted her communicator. "They're not stopping."

"What's the play here? What happens next?"

"I'm supposed to blow up the coupling on this car and our ship tows the train cars away."

Triggs tapped his finger against his right temple for several seconds. "So if we can detach that cable, we scuttle the plan?"

"Yes, I suppose, but how... The pop boxes. We blow the cable instead."

"Do it."

Back outside, they pried pop boxes off the coupling and carried them to the roof.

"Just tie the whole bag to the cable," Triggs said.

Ainsley nodded and pointed down the train. Moving awkwardly in the exoskeleton suit, Francis was jumping the gaps between cars and would be upon them in seconds.

"I'll slow him down. You set the explosives." Triggs ran toward Francis, and Ainsley slipped the pack from her shoulders.

"Ainsley, what the hell are you doing?" Eddie yelled over the comm.

"This isn't the job I signed up for. I'm not letting you take supplies from innocent people."

"What's happening?" Miriam asked.

"I think she's doing something to the clamping cable. I can't see clearly from this far."

"Ainsley, please." When Ainsley didn't answer, Miriam said, "Francis, stop her."

"Francis is occupied. You'll have to get to her. If we lose the heavy cable, I can't pull the train."

"Damn it."

CHAPTER 18

BEN SHOUTED AT the man in the exoskeleton suit. "That suit's not yours. Stand down and give it back, and I won't press charges."

The man's pace slowed for a moment and he yelled, "I can't do that." He resumed his charge, and Ben tried to disable the suit with his wrist computer but he was locked out.

He had thought that would work and realized too late that he didn't have a viable plan B. The man in the suit crossed its mechanical arms in front of himself and rammed into Ben, sending him flying.

The man yelled at Ainsley to stop, but she ignored him.

Ben rolled back to his feet and rammed his shoulder into the man's augmented leg, knocking him to one side but not taking his feet out from under him as Ben had hoped.

The man was inexperienced with an exoskeleton suit and

while he worked to regain his balance, Ben landed two punches in quick succession to his opponent's midsection. When the man pulled his arms in to protect his torso, the big mechanical arms of the suit wrapped around Ben in a painful bear hug.

The man grunted as he tried to make the suit squeeze tighter but the arms were too bulky.

"These things aren't really meant for hand-to-hand combat." Ben wasn't sure why he said it. Maybe it was instinct. If he engaged with dialogue, there was a chance he could de-escalate the situation. The man only grunted and loosened his grip, giving Ben another opening to land a punch at the bottom of the man's ribs. He went for another punch but one of the mechanical hands grabbed Ben's arm and pulled him away, like a child holding a toy away from himself.

He called to Ainsley. "Stop what you're doing or I'll snap the big guy's arm."

Ainsley replied, "This is insane. We said we weren't going to hurt people. "

"I don't want to hurt him, but the job has to get done."

CHAPTER 19

From behind Francis, Miriam appeared on the rooftop.

"If you blow the clamping cable, we'll all be caught. Don't be foolish."

"She's right," Eddie said. "If we lose the big one, the secondary won't hold and you'll be stranded down there."

"Not to add to the stress," Wanda said, "but a security unit is seventy-five seconds out from your position."

"Francis," Eddie shouted, "do what needs to be done."

Before Ainsley could object, Francis flicked the exo suit's mechanical hand and dropped Triggs, who screamed and clutched his arm.

Francis released his hand from the exoskeleton and pulled out the gun wedged between his hip and the suit's restraints.

Aiming at Ainsley, he said, "Don't fret, just a stun slug. We need to finish—"

The exoskeleton popped and Francis fell forward to his hands and knees. The gun slid across the train and fell over the edge. Behind him, Triggs held the emergency release handle in his good hand. Triggs moved around the suit and kicked Francis in the face, sending the fallen man careening sideways.

Ainsley pulled her knot tight to secure the pack and scrambled toward Triggs, scared with each step that she might lose her balance and follow the gun over the edge of the slow-moving train. Francis had curled into a ball to protect himself while Triggs continued to kick him.

"Stop! He's down."

Behind her, the pop boxes exploded and the heavy cable recoiled away from the train, whipping through the air with such force that Ainsley worried it might damage the cargo hauler. A moment later, the thinner secondary cable pulled free from its electromagnetic connection and the ship veered to one side. Both cables dropped out of view.

Eddie said, "I'll circle back and drop a line for Miriam and Francis. Will the big guy let them leave?"

"Thirty seconds," Wanda said.

Ainsley looked Triggs in the eyes. "Yes, they can leave. We won't try to stop them."

Triggs started to say something, but Ainsley held up a hand to quiet him. "I don't want anyone going to a red ship. You know that's what would happen to them."

Eddie flew close and the tether cable dropped from the ship. Francis wrapped it around his chest and tied the cable to itself. He wrapped an arm around Miriam. She clung to him with one hand and to the cable with the other. Blood running from Francis's nose and lip smeared on her arm.

She looked terrified as they rose. They were still swaying in the air when Eddie steered the ship away from the train.

The security ships arrived seconds later. Neither of them chased the cargo hauler. Instead, one pointed its guns at the tiny delivery pod that Triggs must have flown in and the other hovered inches above the train to let a pair of armed guards jump out.

At least they're human, Ainsley thought. Qyntarak guards would have been worse. Not that human guards would mean leniency. She would end up on a red ship, there was little doubt of that. Her last act of service would be to exonerate Triggs. She raised her hands over her head and said to Triggs, "I'm sorry."

The guards said nothing. They lined up their sights and fired.

AINSLEY WOKE WITH her hands tied behind her back. Her collarbone ached from the impact of the stun slug.

Triggs was next to her. His face was wet with tears.

"You alright?" she asked.

"Just a crushed arm."

"Right. Listen, don't worry, I'll tell them everything. You'll be in the clear."

The door opened after several minutes. A bald man moved into the room. He wasn't wearing a uniform but his body language exuded authority.

"Time is short," he said. "You really screwed the pooch, didn't you?"

"Triggs is innocent. It was all me, you can let him go."

"Calm down, Ms. Rosenbaum. Neither of you are in the system yet. There's still an opportunity for redemption for both of you."

"I'm not interested in helping collaborators."

"Nor am I. I'm here on behalf of an organization, well, more than an organization. A movement, let's say, that is working to reclaim Earth for humankind. Your actions today disrupted the acquisition of much needed supplies."

Through gritted teeth, Triggs said, "They were already going to people who needed them."

"You need to broaden your perspective, Mr. Triggs. There are others that need them more. Yes, the shipment was destined for an older exile ship in need of repairs, but the Qyntarak would have resupplied. We, on the other hand, will have a much harder time finding a new source of parts."

"Parts for what?" Ainsley asked.

"We really don't have time for me to explain right now. I only bought us a small window. There are more ways for you to help. We need people like you, people who aren't afraid to act. As I've said, you aren't in the system yet. You could take your chances but you aren't likely to fare well."

"But he's not guilty," Ainsley said. "He was trying to stop the theft."

"That won't matter. The evidence is incriminating. Once you're officially processed, there's little I can do, but there's still time right now for you to be logged as witnesses instead of suspects."

"What do you want in return?" Ainsley asked.

"I'm putting together another team. And it will be right up your alley."

EPILOGUE

RODRIGO SPUN THE anonymous currency token on the table like it was a toy. A very expensive toy. The little device held enough untraceable funds to buy a city block. He daydreamed for a minute about a life in which today's meeting might have been for something as mundane as buying real estate.

He couldn't even imagine.

Instead of a city block, he needed information. And identities for Benjamin Triggs and Esther Rosenbaum. He mustn't forget about them, or Bear and Ainsley as they were choosing to be called now. Stupid names, in his opinion, but he really didn't care. With clean digital IDs in place, they'd be clear to join the new team to smuggle goods onto shipments destined for orbit. Not as strategic as getting the repairs done on the Reclamation's ship, but still important work. And work that would have fewer moral quandaries for them.

The others told him he was living in a fantasy land, but he wasn't ready to abandon hope that Rosenbaum might still be a conduit to get to her parents. Rodrigo had a quota for the number of collaborators he turned. The Rosenbaums would be a nice prize.

The door made a soft grinding sound when it slid open. The noise was probably easy to fix but no one wanted maintenance workers poking around down here. A woman wearing a breathing mask similar to his own entered first. Then the Qyntarak squeezed through the door.

"Assistant Undersecretary."

"Greetings, human Rodrigo." The translator mangled his name as usual, but Rodrigo's pronunciation of the Qyntarak's name was no better.

Rodrigo slid the payment token across the table. "The funds are clean. Enough qynars to grease all the palms."

"Much confusion is in your statement."

"He means the bribes," the woman said as she took the device. "What about the other assignment?"

Rodrigo sat up straighter in his chair. "I've found someone. A researcher doing human-Qyntarak genetic engineering. I think we should pay him a visit."

THE END

If you enjoyed this book, please consider writing a review.

Keep reading for an excerpt from *Weight of Ashes*, the exciting sequel to *Path of Resistance*.

Rook Winters is a tea-fueled writer with a weakness for dad jokes. He lives in New Brunswick, Canada with his family and is definitely a dog person.

Learn more at **rookwinters.com**, follow **@rookwinters on Twitter**, or search for **Rook Winters Author on Facebook**.

GIVING BACK

I have pledged a minimum of ten percent of my proceeds from my books to global relief and development aid. Please join me in supporting the work of organizations that tackle poverty and injustice. If you aren't sure where to give, I recommend **World Vision Canada** for its financial accountability and the integrity of its leadership team.

- Rook

EXCERPT FROM WEIGHT OF ASHES

COURT ADJUSTED THE position of his fingers on his mag gun. Something was in the trees ahead.

Probably a deer. Too quiet for a moose, he thought. Moose would've been a nice treat.

They'd eaten a lot of deer and feral dog lately. They'd be heroes if they brought back a moose.

Beside him, he heard a hint of a wheeze in Walker's breathing. His hay fever was bad this year. Court found it ironic that the kid was allergic to the outdoors given that his people had lived off these lands hundreds of years ago, before the expulsions, before grav tech, before electricity, before anyone had even built cities here.

Court raised the gun and looked over the sight lines at the spot where experience told him the deer would come into view. He saw its head for a fraction of a second. A doe with her ears forward but not facing Court. Something else had her attention. Before he had time to react, the animal bolted.

"What spooked it?" Walker asked.

They heard the answer a moment later. An inorganic sound, something out of place so far from civilization. It was coming from the old road.

"Let's check. But stay out of sight."

They moved faster than they would while stalking prey. Their noise didn't matter compared to the mechanical whining and the sound of fallen branches snapping as something sped along what was once a highway for gas-powered vehicles.

"There." Walker pointed to a two-wheeled machine bouncing over the remains of asphalt mangled by decades of frost heaves.

"That's a motorcycle," Court said. The driver was old like Marsh and the other council members but this man's white beard and hair were neatly trimmed. A smaller passenger sat behind the driver, dressed in black, including a helmet.

"Should we flag them down? They're lost for sure."

"Don't be foolish. We don't want anything to do with city people."

Then Court heard a hum that wasn't from the motorcycle. He grabbed Walker by the shirt and pulled him deeper into the thicket for better cover. It was a sound Court had heard twice before. The first time was with his father on their way home from trading venison for seeds. The second time was a week later when explosives fell on their village. His parents...

Court squeezed his eyes tight. This wasn't the time.

"What's that other sound?"

Court scowled at the younger teen. "It's a gravity control flyer. Shut up and don't move."

The ground under the tangle of bushes was damp. Moisture soaked through the elbows of Court's shirt. It wasn't great cover, and he hoped that whoever was in that flyer only cared about the people on the old motorcycle.

That thing had to be at least fifty years old. It couldn't outrun a grav flyer, especially not driving over a neglected highway that was more footpath than road.

Walker flinched at the sound of a thunderous crack. They couldn't see clearly through the trees but they saw enough. A section of road was sucked into a black dot then spit back out as dust in all directions, leaving a hole the size of a bear in the ground. The leaves around Court and Walker danced as the air reacted to the disruption.

There was no way the old man could avoid the hole but he tried, leaning to his left and jerking the handles. They hit the edge at an angle, launching the passenger from the back. The motorcycle flipped and the man screamed as it crushed his leg.

Walker started to get up and Court clamped his hand on the boy's arm. "Don't move."

The flyer settled a few inches from the ground, hovering over the old asphalt and weeds. It was quiet for something that literally floated in the air. This one looked big enough to hold a half-dozen men but was no louder than a croaking toad. Court could hear the ground crunch under the weight of a Qyntarak as it stepped off.

The sketches and pixelated photos of Qyntarak that Court had seen didn't prepare him for how huge and inhuman they were in real life. This one was twice the size of the man it was bearing down upon. Its four spindly legs supported a long body that curved up and then hung down at the end, like a branch bearing too much fruit. It wore body armor and cradled what Court guessed was a weapon in its two shortest arms, the ones that looked most like human arms with finger-like parts. Its other arm equivalents, two long ones with pointed ends and two shorter ones with blunt pincers, were fanned out like tree branches made of snakes.

He'd once heard Qyntarak compared to giant centipedes crossed with spiders crossed with horses, but that comparison was inadequate because it didn't capture how alien they looked. Court knew that underneath that body armor, there was nothing resembling a face.

"Dr. Donovan," the monster said, its voice synthetic and unnatural through the speakers of its body armor, "you left the compound without authorization. Guilt of desertion is upon you."

The man, Donovan, wiped blood from his mouth and said something in a language Court didn't recognize.

"The governor has a message for you."

A long moment passed in silence then a different but equally synthetic voice said, "Donovan, friend of many years, the disappointment you have created in me is great. Your actions are foolish gestures. This failure brings shame to me. It was selfish of you."

Donovan uttered something else in the unknown language. Then in English he said, "You are the fool. The human spirit cannot be contained. Oligarchies never last. Empires always fall."

"Your time has expired. Others will resume your work and you will be forgotten. You have accomplished nothing but to bring cold to my mandibles. Goodbye."

The alien moved forward. "Traitor."

Another crack, this time quieter.

The Qyntarak returned to its flyer and it shot upward with a deep hum.

Walker began to move again but Court kept his grip on him and shook his head no. They waited until the hum was gone and the chirping of birds resumed. Cautiously, they moved to the road. The old man was lying on his back with a hole in his chest almost as large as his head. What was left of his torso was covered in gray powder. Blood oozed and mixed with it, creating a sludge in the cavity.

Walker steadied himself against a tree and vomited.

"You alright?"

"I'm fine."

"Where's the other one?"

After a brief search, they found the body, stiff and unmoving, among the trees at the edge of the road.

"It's a girl," Walker said. "Or a woman, I guess."

She wore a dull black bodysuit with no visible seams or fasteners. Her helmet was solid with no visor or eyeholes. Court pressed his fingers against her neck and then her wrist.

"The suit's cold. I can't feel a pulse through it, and I don't see how to remove it."

"We can cut it open with my hunting knife."

"No, not out here. We need to get them closer to the village and find Marsh. He'll know what to do."

Court was weeks away from his twentieth birthday, almost a year since he became a full adult in the village, and even though the fourteen-year-old Walker thought the older teen knew everything, Court was well aware of how much he didn't know. Like what to do with two dead bodies.

"We'll push them on the motorcycle," he said.

They followed the road for nearly a kilometer to where a dry creek bed reached the road. It was slow moving with the bodies draped over the bike. Blood trickled from the dead man and Court worried that it might attract coywolves or a bear. He didn't say anything to Walker. If the kid was worried, he wasn't showing it.

With considerable effort, they pushed the bike far enough up the creek to be out of sight of the road. The road wasn't frequently traveled but that didn't mean it was wise for Court to linger there with the bodies while Walker fetched Marsh.

It would take the better part of an hour for Walker to return. Court sat on the ground and rested against a maple tree with his mag gun in his lap. It was a beautiful day. Late summer or early fall, depending on one's point of view. A day too beautiful for death and dying.

Eventually, Court heard the crunch-crunch-tap of Marsh with his walking stick and stood to meet the village council leader.

"Where are they?" Marsh said, forgoing the normal pleasantries of conversation that he'd drilled into Court for years.

"There."

Marsh stopped several feet away and brought his free hand to his chest. "Clint." He knelt and put his hand on the man's face. "I don't understand."

"You know him?"

"Knew him, yes. A long time ago. Clint Donovan. He was a researcher. Became a collaborator to avoid exile."

Walker asked, "What about the woman?"

"Impossible to say with that helmet."

"We couldn't find any obvious way to take it off," Court said. "I didn't dare take a knife to the suit."

Marsh felt around the woman's wrist and elbow. "Wise choice. It might be booby trapped." He studied the suit and helmet for another minute. "Try pressing Clint's hand against the front of the helmet."

Walker looked like he might be sick again as they rolled the body and lined up the dead man's hand over the helmet and pressed it down. The helmet clicked and air hissed as a seam appeared. The woman's hand twitched and Walker yelped. Her arm knocked him off balance as her hands flew to the helmet. She pushed it open, two curved panels sliding to the sides as if on invisible tracks.

***

Weight of Ashes is available now in print and ebook